The Gravedigger's Cottage

ALSO BY CHRIS LYNCH

Shadow Boxer
Iceman
Gypsy Davey
Political Timber
Slot Machine
Extreme Elvin
Whitechurch

The Blue-Eyed Son Trilogy:
Mick
Blood Relations
Dog Eat Dog

Gold Dust
Freewill
All the Old Haunts
Who the Man

The Gravedigger's Cottage

CHRIS LYNCH

 HarperCollins*Publishers*

Library of Congress Cataloging-in-Publication Data
Lynch, Chris.
The gravedigger's cottage / Chris Lynch.—1st ed.
    p.   cm.
Summary: When fourteen-year-old   Sylvia
McLuckie, her ten-year-old brother Walter, and
their quirky father move to a cottage by the sea,
their new home's eerie reputation forces them to
confront some surprising ghosts from their past.
ISBN 0-06-623940-0 — ISBN 0-06-623941-9 (lib.
bdg.)
[1. Brothers and sisters—Fiction. 2. Fathers—
Fiction. 3. Family problems—Fiction. 4. Moving,
Household—Fiction. 5. Seashore—Fiction.] I.
Title.
PZ7.L979739 Gr 2004   2003013961
[Fic]—dc22   CIP
                                                      AC

Typography by Amy Ryan
1 2 3 4 5 6 7 8 9 10
❖
First Edition

To Fran Lebowitz,
who made me what I am today,
and then fled the scene of the crime

Sea Grass

My dad always says he doesn't live in a country, he lives in a house. He doesn't live in a town or a village, he lives in a house. He sure doesn't live in any neighborhood. He lives in, you know, a house.

I live in a house. I also live in a house near the sea, but not right *staring* at the sea. You don't need to be staring at the sea to be at the sea, feeling and absorbing and living the sea.

In fact, I have this idea that you could do away with all the individual senses of the sea—the smell of it and the salt taste in the air and the smash of the waves—and still, without any clues, somehow you would know you were at the sea. Just because it is such a *thing*, the sea.

I live in a house, by the sea.

But I also live in a country, in a village, and in a

neighborhood, and that matters.

And in the house I live in there are two guys, my dad and my little brother, Walter, who is ten. I am the lady of the house, and I am fourteen. I'm Sylvia.

Nobody calls me Sylvie. Sylvia's my name, it's the name I was given, it's the name I like. It's me. My dad calls me Vee, which I like, but mostly from him or from Walter but not really from anybody else— though nobody else has really attempted it yet. Probably that's for the best all around.

Now here's the thing about Walter. We are more alike than you would expect a fourteen-year-old girl and a ten-year-old boy to ever be. We are the same, practically, or anyway as same as anybody can be with a ten-year-old boy. Which is to say we are different. Very, very different.

But different only in the obvious ways, none of the unobvious ways, and absolutely none of the important ways. We think alike. Which is to say, he is a good little thinker there, my Walter. We are so alike because we have all that same stuff inside us and behind us and all around us. We have been there, together, and we are still there, together. I like the way he thinks. He's got a good brain.

But I could never tell him that. That would spoil it.

My dad likes to sit in his chair, and he likes to go to flea markets on the weekends and look at other people's chairs. And he likes large multipacks of thick white socks that don't have the seam running right across the front bumper of his toes. Soft thick socks that have the seam in the right place make my dad feel nice, and the other kind make him feel not at all nice; and he likes to live completely within his nice cozy socks, within his nice cozy house.

And we want him feeling nice. He doesn't feel nice quite enough of the time, Dad doesn't.

Which is not to say that he is not nice. He is the nicest dad you ever met. He just doesn't *feel* nice. So probably you might wonder how I would know how a person *feels* if he doesn't talk about how he feels, which is exactly what my dad does not talk about. Probably you'd be wondering how I'd know that.

"Because she knows *everything*, that's how. Because she is *Sylvia*, and she knows everything."

That's what Walter would say. But he wouldn't mean it in a good way, in case you were wondering. But I would thank him anyway.

"Thank you, Walter."

"I was being sarcastic."

"But I love *you*." This would drive him nuts.

"Don't *start* that, Sylvia."

"But I love *you*."

"You know . . ." he'd say to me, but I already would know he wouldn't finish his thought, "you know, Sylvia . . ."

"I know," I'd say, as he stomped away.

Anyway, he was kind of right about me knowing feelings just because I do. Mostly, though, I know my dad's feelings. And so does Walter. We watch him and watch over him. That is our job, to watch over him and see to him, and to allow him to watch over us and see to us.

It is a good system. Everybody benefits.

Even if I do most of the work. That's to be expected. I'm the woman of the house.

But that's okay. It's nice to be needed. Everybody wants to be needed.

Our house, the house that we recently moved into, sits in a little sand flea of a coastal village. It's not a highly happening place where people move to all the time, but my dad's work had been asking him to move here about once a year for a few years. Guess they were having trouble staffing this particular office. My dad is a financial guy, which means I have no idea what he does all day. But according to him, he is a "small-business terrifier," going in and scaring them into showing him their records. I told him I thought that was sad. He told me he agreed.

Anyway, our house. The Gravedigger's Cottage is what it's called. Everyone we met in the first days after we got here, from the mailman to the electric meter reader to the cashier in the local store, spoke to us with a mix of real fear and admiration when they informed us that we had taken up residence in the famous Gravedigger's Cottage, aka The Diggers. But no one could make a half-decent attempt at telling us why the house was known as the Gravedigger's Cottage. The person who sold it to us was a retired schoolteacher, not a gravedigger.

Which was not any big deal except that this gravedigger business started to attach itself, like a big ugly sucker fish, to us. Somehow the locals decided that the legend of the Gravedigger's Cottage had something to do with the people who had lived there for sixteen days, rather than any of the occupants who had taken lukewarm baths there—the hot water was the lamest part of the house—for the previous hundred years or so.

Which I thought was rather unfair.

It bothered Walter a lot right from the start that kids would call us the Diggerkids. They would run or ride up to our hedge, yelling clever stuff like "Dig it!" or "Diggers!" and then be gone by the time we got to the window or the door. It bothered Walter way more when they called our dad the Gravedigger.

Walter began keeping a small collection of perfect throwing rocks in a beach pail by his bedroom window.

I wouldn't go that far myself. But I didn't like it that they were calling my dad the Gravedigger. No, I didn't like that. My dad, the Gravedigger. If ever there were proof that whoever runs life has a nasty sense of humor, that was it.

My dad bought this house I think more for the sea grass than for any other single thing. Surely he bought it for the actual sea, which was nearby, and for its quirky weirdness—it is a long and low L-shaped white stone thing laid out all on one floor, except for the gabled bedrooms above—and for the garage. He likes garages and all the stuff you can stuff in them and appears unaware that there is any connection between them and automobiles. When I suggested that it would be nice to park the car in the garage, he responded that having a car in a garage was like having a toilet in the kitchen—two perfectly useful things that spoil each other. And that, pretty much, settled that.

But mostly I think he bought the place for the sea grass, for the tall ruggedy hedge, and for the apple trees.

We have two of them. Seashore apple trees, Dad calls them, and he is as proud of them as if they were our very own twisted, leafy brothers.

Have you ever tasted those apples? Those luminous lime-colored, bumpy, knotted, gnarly apples that live on the salted air and thin earth of the seaside? They are very special apples, with a character, Dad insists, that comes out of their hard life facing into mean North Atlantic winds all the time. "Mighty special" is Dad's way of describing those apples. Before this year, he always drove us everywhere, hunting down those weird little apples—and the truth is, Walter and I were always a little disappointed to find them.

And now they are growing in our very yard. "Unlike anything else you are ever likely to taste," Dad pronounced loudly when he first stood under his very own fruit tree.

"And a good thing too," Walter pronounced not so loudly. Walter cannot stand the kind of apples that come off our very own trees.

But every year after our apple-picking trips, we ate the pie and the applesauce and apple butter and apple jelly and whatever all Dad could squeeze out of the crop and his evil *Old New England Harvesttime* book of ideas; and now that the trees were our very own, we could be sure of many bitter harvests to come.

Dad enjoys his apples. Even if, if I'm honest, I will tell you that they seem to be apples that were never intended to be eaten by humans. He enjoys all apples because he is apple mental.

And hedges and sea grass, those too. We have a big seven-foot hedge that runs here and there sporadically all around our property, trying hard to separate the house from the world and establish where we begin and everything else ends. It is a game old hedge, but sloppy and ragged enough to leave spaces for the truly curious to have a peek. And at the back of the property, where the garage meets the hedge, there is a little natural walkway, a strange but fantastic miniature sand-dune scene all our own, where we have a mysterious long and deep layer of the most silky white beach sand you ever saw, and out of it is growing the tallest, heartiest, stalkiest crop of beach grass that ever grew. It serves as an escort, a regal green honor guard as we drive the long unplanned and unpaved driveway to our house, our home, our private cozy little Gravedigger's Cottage far off the main road from everything at all. It is about two hundred yards, I'd say, from the spot where you turn off the road to where you pass right by our garage for anything but cars, to where you drive up almost all the way through our backyard to bump up to the back of the house.

And the whole way, it is like we are in some kind of parade or attending a big movie opening. Taller and taller the grasses get, brushing the sides of the car, reaching up over the fender, over the window glass, the wispy fingers of the green and gold sea grass stroking us with their tough razor stalks and their feathery light tips. Caressing us and ushering us home, all the way until we are all the way in, at the Gravedigger's Cottage and nowhere else. Out of

the country, out of the town, out of the neighborhood, and into the house.

It fits Dad's idea of having a home. He never cared
one way or another for possessing things, never
quite believed it was possible. He subscribes to the
theory of negative ownership, meaning the place you
own can never really be yours, be fully a part of you,
but your owning it really just means you're the only
one with the undeniable right to be there.

And the rest of the universe can't come inside
without your say-so.

The trees, the hedges, the sea grass, the distance
between the back door and the rest of the world. I
think Dad was sold on the house before he ever even
went inside it.

McLuckie

We don't talk about our mothers a great deal. There were two of them, one mine and one Walter's. Two Mrs. McLuckies.

I know, but it's true. There was a time, when I was just getting mature, when I doubted it myself. It suddenly occurred to me that it might have been a bizarre joke, that that wasn't our name at all, since how could anybody have a name like that in real life, especially if they had been fairly spectacularly not so lucky? So I looked it up on the Internet. A very Scottish name, apparently. Traceable back hundreds of years to a settlement on the Isle of Mull. Lucky enough to have gotten off a place with a name like Mull, I suppose.

So I am Sylvia McLuckie, just as my mother was Sylvia McLuckie before me. Walter is Walter

McLuckie, and Dad is Mr. McLuckie.

And, back then, there were the two Mrs. McLuckies, within four years of each other. And then there were none.

There hasn't been another one since. Not even close.

I don't know that I would even want another one, myself. And I definitely don't know if I would want one if I were Dad. How hard must that have been, to lose so much so early? And then again, so soon?

I don't know, really. It's easier for a baby to lose something. It has to be. But what about a man? A husband, a dad? What about that?

I wouldn't know because, like I said, we don't talk a great deal about the two Mrs. McLuckies. About the missing Mrs. McLuckies. I never specifically heard my dad talk about how it felt to lose them both. Better to have loved and lost than never to have loved at all, is what the saying says. But I doubt if whoever said it had ever loved and lost so much so quickly.

I think you might choose not loving at all.

But while there is no Mrs. McLuckie III, you could not say there is no love. My dad can love stuff.

He loves, like I said, socks and chairs. Apples. Everything related to the seaside, while not necessarily the open sea. Privacy. He loves wind and rain but not snow. Food. One-star movie reviews. He enjoys those nasty reviews about as much as most people enjoy four-star movies. And he loves nearly empty old movie theaters when it's a matinee and they're playing a one-star movie. Tea he loves, both the normal Earl Grey kind and the herbal tea that doesn't even taste like anything.

And us. Me and Walter. He loves us just about as much as it is possible. I wonder sometimes if he has so much stored up in his tank for my brother and me because he was never allowed to spend much of it on our mothers. I wonder that.

Things Die

I know things die.

"You make them die."

"Shut up, Walter."

"Dad doesn't like you telling me to shut up, Sylvia."

"Well, he doesn't like you making me feel like a ghoul either."

"Well, you do make things die, Vee. You just do."

"Shut *up*. I don't *make* them die. They just die. Things die, Walter. Everything dies."

"But you speed things up a little."

He's being quite unfair.

"Yah? Who killed the hamster then, Walter?"

"Don't."

"Remember the hamster, Walter? Remember Vladimir?"

"Stop it, Sylvia. That was different."

"Yah, it was different because it was murder, and mine were all accidents."

"It was not murder! It was love. I *loved* Vladimir to death, and you know it. I didn't know any better. I was only little. I thought he was like any other stuffed animal."

"Remember his eyes? Remember when you squeezed so hard his eyes—"

"Dad!"

He did. He squeezed that poor hamster into the next world like toothpaste out of a tube, and I know he didn't know what he was doing, but is that enough to get you off the hook? Does that make it any more okay, because he didn't know what he was doing? I think most stuff happens because people don't know what they are doing—to animals or to themselves or to other people—but does that mean that the same stuff hasn't happened, once it has happened? Stuff is always happening, but I never notice it un-happening, and hardly anybody seems to know what they're doing.

Walter is right; I've buried a lot of pets.

"It's why we had to move."

"It is not why we had to move. We moved for Dad's work."

"We had to move because there was no more land

left where we were before. Your pet cemetery sur-
rounding our house was finally all filled up, every
inch. They said we were a health hazard with all the
rotting animals in our yard. Everybody was afraid
the ground was going to come bubbling up with the
bodies of all these dogs and turtles and birds and
everything, like a scene from a pet zombie horror
movie. The people of the town came to our door late
one night, with torches—"

This did not happen. Walter is a boy, and he's ten,
and so he says things like that. He's programmed to
be a jerk.

"Dad doesn't like it when you call me names."

"Dad isn't listening. Perhaps you should do likewise."

You want to know all about my mom, probably.

I'd like to know that myself.

I lied. I wouldn't like to know. It doesn't bother me
anymore. I swear. She is not here because she has
never been here, and that's just all right. All right
with me. She was gone almost when I first woke up,
you know, woke up to the world; and like anything
that's not there when you first wake up you can't
very well miss it. Same goes for Walter's mom, my
second mom. I was still wiping my eyes practically,
waking up and calming down at the same time from
what happened the first time, and there it happened

again. Poor Walter never even knew what hit him. Poor Walter. Poor, lucky Walter. Can't miss what you never knew, can you?

Except you can, of course. You can miss. You can and you do miss, and if I lied you would know, so I will try not to lie to you.

But I told the truth at the same time as lying . . .

Both at the same time. I don't miss my mom, exactly, because I didn't know her. Much. I'm sure she was lovely. I mean, I have seen pictures, of course, and she was lovely. Very, very lovely to look at.

And I have no doubt she was also lovely on the inside. I am sure she could hold a kid on her knee and clean scrapes without making them hurt worse. I am sure she could sing. I am sure she smelled like strawberry or patchouli or Oil of Olay, if that is an actual smell. I'm sure she read out loud at bedtime and had a purse full of lipstick and Kleenex and butterscotch candies and Wash 'n Dri moist towelettes for emergencies. I'm sure she could cook. I'm sure she could sing. I know I already said that, but just then I was thinking that she would be singing while she was cooking, and so I said it again because it occurred to me again. I hope you don't mind. I don't think you do. I bet she was a very careful driver, and courteous. I bet she was a good swimmer. I bet she would go into the pool and swim with us, no matter that a lot of parents don't go into the pools and I think it is because they are self-conscious about their flabby parental bodies. Although I know she had a lovely figure. I saw it in a picture. I bet her taste in clothes was excellent.

So, you see. Those are the things I think. There are more, of course, but you get the picture, and I don't want to try and give any more of that picture. The point just being, I would miss my mom if I knew all that about her firsthand, from memory. I would miss her, and all the things about her—the inside, outside, everything of her. I would miss them every day, forever.

Maybe it hurts less then, if you are done the small favor of losing somebody too soon. Before you get to know too much. Maybe. Maybe it hurts less then. Maybe. Maybe that's why I don't miss my mom too specifically.

Generally, though, there's a different story. That mom space with nothing in it? That hurts probably as much as a hundred real moms could ever hurt you. But, like I said, that's another story, and that's not the story I was meaning to tell.

The story I was meaning to tell was the story of one of the last things that happened at the old house before we moved to the Gravedigger's Cottage. And, yes, of course it is about a dying, like most stories eventually are, and a burying in the crowded patch of land around that sorry old place.

Loose Lucy got hit by a car. We buried her in the northeast corner of the yard in the shade of a triangle of hedge but underneath a bright streetlight that shines right down on her once the sun sets. Walter joked that she can't tell day from night now because of that, and Dad said she was only barely able to tell day from night before, which was partly how she wound up in the ground after all.

She was a love. But he is right. She was far more heart than head. Loose—as in, her bolts were never really tightened up all the way.

It seems to me like everybody in the world has one of those stories, one of those hit-by-car stories about their dogs, or former dogs or cats or whatever. I didn't used to think about it. I think about it all the time now, because I see it now, like I didn't before, and I feel it now. Everybody was always so okay when they told these stories: Rusty got run over, Sheeba got run over, Alf got run over. They were so awfully *okay* about it when they said it. Right—they were all sad enough, all a little embarrassed and guilty and all. But they were intact. They were not wrecked. They got on with things and told the tale, as if having a flu shot or having a tooth pulled was pretty much the same hurt as watching two tons of truck flatten thirty pounds of best friend.

It is *not* the same feeling. It feels horrible. I mean,

horrible. How can people talk about it like it's anything else?

Because if you've seen it and heard it—god, if you've heard it—it would get you forever.

The tires screeched. Exactly the same pitch as Loose Lucy screeched once she caught on to what was happening to her. It was as if she were matching a pitch pipe, starting out with a bark-yelp-yowl-howl, all of it swooshing together until she got both lungs into it and screamed. Screamed. Like a *person*, she screamed like a *person*, finally, when they are *dying*, and they just then learn to tell you what is inside them, and then they are gone. Ah, Lucy. My Lucy.

The truck was jamming its brakes; the driver was shifting through the gears, down, trying to slow it and stop it and reverse it. I was wishing, like the driver was certainly wishing, that he could reverse this whole thing. Loose Lucy surely would have been wishing we could reverse, if she could imagine reverse. If she could imagine wishing.

But Loose Lucy, poor simple Lucy, couldn't imagine something as complicated as wishing, and none of us could imagine reversing time and awfulness. And so she was dead. Good and dead.

Why do people say that? Good and dead. That's just stupid.

Bad and dead.

She got all bent up, poor Lucy. Her back legs

twisted up one way while the front were aiming another, as if this were two different parts of different dogs just passing each other on their way to two whole different places.

"Sorry, sorry, Lucy," I kept saying, because it was my fault. She was never supposed to be out off the leash for just this reason. I only wanted to let her run, just for a minute, just for then. I did it before, just for a minute, and it worked out all right. And if you ever saw her, saw how excited she was, running, you would see why I would want to do that for her. You would want to do that for her, I know you would.

"Sorry, sorry, I am so sorry, Luce," I said, as I held her head and she stared off past my right shoulder, as if I were up there, my head up there high above my right shoulder rather than tightly attached to my neck where I usually keep it.

There was a little blood puddled up in the middle of Lucy's tongue, in the middle of her strange white gums. It wasn't a lot of blood. There was a little more from a three-inch slash on her leg, but that wasn't much either. Should have been more, but it was almost as if someone had run the tap of Loose Lucy's blood and then snapped it shut again just as quick. Her belly was swelling.

She tried to get up. Half of her tried. The front half tried, but it was a weak try. I guided her head back down to the ground where she lay, and she didn't fight me. She looked grateful to be there, lying down on the ground again, as if she never would have thought of that if I hadn't pointed it out. That was very Lucy of her, I thought, and I was grateful that she was being very Lucy for me.

And then she did it—went and died. She closed her little eyes, and she stopped the short whispery pant she was doing; she let her tongue just flop there, touching the pavement with the very tip, like you would do if you were testing something out, soup or something, if you were afraid it was going to be too hot yet.

"I'm sorry," the man said, as soon as he was sure Lucy had left. We were the only two people there yet, me and the truck driver. There would be lots others soon enough, but for this, it was just us. "I am very sorry," he said again, and he didn't try to explain anything away even though it was not his fault. "I am so sorry," he said again, shaking his head, looking at Lucy, shaking his head. I felt so sorry for him, seeing his face, seeing this big guy, this big nine-foot-tall truck driver guy, seeing him go all crackly faced, and it just got worse when he leaned over past me and put his plaid shirt down over Lucy, as if we could still keep her warm, keep her wrapped, keep any more of her from seeping out and away.

"I'm sorry, mister," I said, looking up at him, but staying crouched low to stroke Lucy. "I'm not supposed to let her off the leash, ever . . . I'm sorry . . ."

That was when I started to cry. And then that was when the truck driver started doing not so well himself, and I got a whole lot worse when I saw him, not crying exactly, but coming I guess as close as one of these big nine-foot men probably comes.

I turned away from the bright glassy eyes on that man, bright glassy shiny eyes where I could swear for a flash I was sure I saw us reflected. The picture of me and Lucy on the ground, her helpless, me useless. I turned from him and buried myself, laid my whole face right down into the neck part of my Lucy, just below her folded velvet ear, where she used to let you nuzzle for hours, and I nuzzled her for maybe hours, at least until I felt my dad's hands squeezing my shoulders, warming me and comforting me and making me start to wail harder than ever.

She was already all stiff when we put her down in the corner of the yard a few hours later. I couldn't believe it. Already. Already going and gone and taken away. Rigid, like she was already not our Lucy who would fetch oranges across this same yard, but a stuffed museum version of our Lucy. Her closed eyes were kind of pulling in, like she was squinting them, holding them tight against seeing what was going on and maybe then keeping it from going on.

Nice try, Luce. Hold 'em closed tight and maybe

see something better.

Dad scooted up next to me at the foot of Loose Lucy's grave. He had an arm draped over my shoulder. His fingernails were packed with the rich clay dirt of the digging, and his shirt was moist with sweat. The smell of him made me feel comfortable and right in a very sad way. This was the smell, to me, of saying good-bye.

I would know that smell, wouldn't I? I was doing this all the time, killing things. Unless it was them doing it to me, dying. All the same, in the end, they ended up there, under there, under us, with the earth upturned and the scent penetrating all the way into me and staying there.

Walter had stood by the grave now for as long as he was able to do any one thing. He had been okay through this, resisting his natural urge to upset me and to pretend he didn't feel hurt. Without speaking, he went into the house.

He didn't see me see him, but I saw him raise his eyes and tell her good-bye.

"What are you thinking, Sylvie?" Dad asked.

Two things. One, for starters, he didn't ever call me Sylvie, like I said. He was trying to play. He was trying to help. I loved it when he tried.

The other thing was, he knew better than to ask that. We had been through this many times before, with him asking me what was I thinking.

I never answered that. Because I *said* what I was thinking when I wanted to talk about what I was thinking. I had no trouble saying, when I wanted to be saying, but when I didn't want to be saying, you could tell, because I stood there, *not* saying. Because I think that's important. I think your thoughts are more like a place, where you can stay, comfortably alone if need be.

But he asked, and I told him. I told him all that, or at least I used to tell him all that, all those first few thousand times he asked me what I was thinking, but now I had shortened the whole thing to a special one-word digest: "*Dad,*" which was pronounced with two distinct syllables, "*Da-ad,*" and he remembered right away and then we were okay again. Then, usually a little while later when I was quiet again, he would ask me again what I was thinking and I would patiently tell him again. And then he'd remember again. And then we were okay again.

"Well, you want to know what I'm thinking, then?" he said as he gently steered me away from our good-bye to Loose Lucy as darkness began to really finally close us in.

"Yah, Dad, I do."

"I'm thinking I'm really looking forward to the new house, to a new start. I'm thinking we were here long enough. I'm thinking it's time."

He squeezed me extra hard, and as we approached

the back door we saw the backlit figure of Walter standing in the doorway, arms folded, as if we had been out all night and kept him up worrying.

"Yah, Dad," I said, leaning into him, "I'm thinking you're right."

This was the first I had heard of this thought. But it must have been true because I said it.

Same went for this one.

"And I'm thinking I don't want any more pets, once we get to the new house. I'm thinking I couldn't bear to bury anything else under us, at the new place."

He let this go without remark. He gave my shoulder a silent squeeze. Much went without remark with Dad, but sometimes the silent squeeze wasn't what I wanted. Sometimes it was, but I had a right to a choice, didn't I?

"Doesn't it hurt, Dad? Doesn't it keep hurting, even when it's past? And doesn't it want to come out sometimes?"

He did it. He had the nerve to squeeze my shoulder again. When I kept staring up at him, heating up the side of his face with my glare, he was forced to consider again.

"It'll be okay, sweetheart," was what he decided, was what he always decided. "We won't dwell on that now," was what he said next, as he always liked to say next.

"Right." I sighed as we stepped inside. As we did,

Dad grabbed Walter in a one-arm bear hug, while still holding me with the other. When we were squished way up close together, I leaned over and kissed Walter on his big round forehead.

"Hey!" Walter shouted.

He didn't really mind though. It beat what he was doing, in the house, alone with his red-rimmed eyes.

Welcome

Among the many kinks of the Gravedigger's Cottage was the doorbell, which made a clang sound as if someone were hitting one of the radiators with a great big hammer.

The first time I heard it, it threw me a little, but then it was nothing compared to what I found outside the door when I answered.

"Hi," I said.

"I'll be your boyfriend," he said.

We had never met. We had lived in the house for about a week. It was August, school hadn't started yet, Dad hadn't gone back to work. We spent our time, the three of us, nicing up the house some, visiting the rocky, fairly private beach, and puttering about the general vicinity without really meeting people in any meaningful way. And then came Carmine.

"Um, you will not be my boyfriend, no."

"Wow, you're mean," he said.

"I am not mean. Who *are* you?"

"I'm Carmine."

"Hi, Carmine. Thanks but—"

I was forced to interrupt myself here because of what Carmine was doing while I talked. While I talked, he wrapped himself up in a hug as if he were worrying or cold, which in eighty-two-degree heat was unlikely.

"Why are you doing that?" I asked.

"What?" He kept doing it.

"Stop that," I said, pointing at his huggy arms. There was a daffy excited smile that went along with the hug.

Walter heard and came to the door.

"Hey, Carmine," Walter said.

Carmine stopped the hugging and turned sort of normal looking. "Hi, Walter."

"How do you know him?" I asked Walter.

"Ah-o-o."

Walter answered me the way he had answered almost every direct question since he'd turned ten, with a stretched-out single syllable sluurb that contained all the elements of the words *I don't know* without actually articulating any of them. *Ah-o-o.* Sometimes he managed it without even opening his mouth, and it still sounded the same.

Fortunately or unfortunately, I spoke the language.

"How can you not know? How can you meet somebody, how can you know somebody, and not know how?"

Bet you could guess what his answer was.

"So who have we got here?" Dad said, completing the whole happy family in the doorway.

"I'm her boyfriend," Carmine said. Then he hugged himself.

"You are *what*?" Dad said in such a different voice from the friendly greeting of a few seconds earlier, I had to turn and check that it was still him.

"He is *not*," I said to Dad. "You are *not*," I said to Carmine.

Walter was beginning to gather how upsetting I was finding this, and acted accordingly. "Don't be mean, Sylvia," he said. "Loosen up."

"Yes," Carmine said, "loosen up."

"Do not loosen up," Dad said.

"I used to have a friend who lived in this house," Carmine said.

"Really?" I said. "Well, you don't now."

"Yes, he does—me," said Walter.

"How did the two of you meet?" asked Dad.

"*Ah-o-o*," they both said; they both shrugged.

It went on this way for a while before Carmine was invited into the house. It was by no means a unanimous decision, with Walter wanting him in, me wanting him gone, and Dad ultimately I think just wanting him off our front step.

"Wow," Carmine said as he stepped into the front hallway and past the fifteen-pane glass foyer door. "What a cool house."

"I thought you had friends here before?" I said.

"Yah," he said, looking around as if he were in a museum, "but they moved away a few years ago. And they never let me inside."

I whipped around and laid a *see* stare on Walter.

Walter made his other universal response noise. "Huh?"

He was our first house tour. I was thinking about it even as we were doing it, traipsing like a tiny indoor parade through the odd-size doorways, into the odd-shaped rooms, how weird the idea was. Why should anybody else care what your house looks like? Why should anybody think that it was a good and pleasant and entertaining idea to be dragged around and shown somebody else's bedroom and pantry and toilet? I had never conducted one of those tours before, had never been taken on one, and, frankly, never missed it.

Carmine couldn't have agreed less.

"What an amazing door," he said as we slipped from the foyer into the living room. It was a nice enough door—tall and rectangular; bare, scratchy, cocoa-colored wood that had once been painted lilac but was now stripped clean except for some artfully overlooked patches. Nice enough but amazing? You had to be pretty excitable.

And that was Carmine.

"Look at the bite marks!" he squealed. There was evidence all over the house that the previous occupants kept cats or badgers or macaques that were allowed total freedom. It was kind of cool in spots, kind of gross in others. Carmine took advantage of the situation to make a grab for my hand, to comfort one or the other of us. Bless him.

"Want to see a lot more bite marks?" I said.

The hand troubled me no more.

It was almost like we were seeing the house new again, as if *we* were the ones being shown around. Because this was different from when the real estate woman had shown the place to us. Even though it was only a very short time ago, it was very different.

Because it was ours now. It was, already, us.

And it was so very, very much a *cottage*. We were living in a cottage.

I had always connected the word *cottage* with a kind of sweetness, a quaint, temporary, novelty type of structure. I never thought of a cottage as being a place where people—human people, serious, full-size, nonfictional people—would ever live, full-time, all the time.

Neither did the previous owners, apparently.

There was a lot of homemade about the place. The doors to both my bedroom and Walter's were a lot closer to picnic tabletops than real doors. They didn't even have knobs but instead had those little kind of garden gate latches that you opened with a flick up of a finger. The natural wood floor of the living room was a darkish molasses color, except for four or five wide boards, positioned randomly here and there. These were a dramatically different blond wood, apparently used to replace old bad boards.

Except then when you went into Dad's bedroom, across the hall, the floor all over was a brilliant blond wood—except for four or five randomly placed molasses boards, matching the living room floor.

"It's like a puzzle," Carmine said with delight.

Dad, I noticed, was looking at it all anew. And with something less than delight. His brow crunched down low over his eyes as he concentrated on what he was seeing, and he started acting like some kind of hired surveyor of his own place. He drew his famous little notebook out of his right hip pocket. And his trusty little pen from the left front.

Walter looked at me, and I at him. Dad was taking notes.

"Can I go to the bathroom?" Carmine asked, the excitement proving too much for his system.

"Sure," Walter said, failing to read Dad's face.

Dad's face, if you cared to read it, clearly stated that it was time for Carmine to go home and use his own bathroom.

He is not impolite, my dad. Far from it. It was just that, even before now we had become aware of what was probably the house's least charming eccentricity.

The toilet was not the most robust mechanism. You could all but hear it sigh with fatigue and depression when you flushed it.

Up till now it was an annoyance, but at least it hadn't been a public nuisance. This was the world getting inside our soft underbelly, and Dad would have problems with that.

Now . . .

We mulled, almost huddled around the bathroom door, as we waited for Carmine to return to the tour. The bathroom was situated at the far tip of the L by the back door just off the kitchen. It was not an out-of-the-way place. It was not a through way. It was not a place we could cut the tour and leave somebody who—despite claiming to have friends who used to live here—did not know his way around.

So we waited. Nearby.

Dad made busy, turning on the loud kettle to make tea whether we wanted it or not. Walter went shopping in the fridge, staring, closing it, opening it, staring. I turned on the kitchen radio for the camouflage of music, but timed it just right for *Story Time*, which they might as well call nap time.

It was all a kind of hoax anyway. We were not trying not to listen. We were trying not to *seem* to be listening.

Meanwhile we were listening our heads off.

And rooting for the toilet.

Come on, toilet.

Walter slid up next to me, whispering. "What is he doing all this time?"

"I don't know. He's *your* little friend."

"He's *your* boyfriend."

"I am going to kill the next person who—"

We were interrupted, fortunately, by the sounds of some telltale rustling in the bathroom. A shuffling of feet, a big slam of the seat . . .

Come on, toilet.

Dad, try though he might to be cool about it, was leaning his whole self in the direction of that bathroom door, like a silent movie guy leaning into the wind.

We were perhaps putting a lot of pressure on the poor toilet to uphold the family honor.

The toilet let us down.

Oh my. Oh, that wasn't very good at all. The toilet . . . it wasn't even all the toilet's fault in all fairness. That little Carmine must have just waved at the handle, because the thing didn't even manage its usual sad swish of a flush. It was like it had quit and died right there, with all its steam running out. If you could punch a toilet unexpectedly in the stomach, this is the sound it'd make.

You'd have to understand about Dad, and his privacy, and his ways with people and the world and all. He didn't go out into the world more than he had to, and he didn't let the world come inside much either. So something like this, like Carmine coming in and getting *toured*, well, that was big effort for Dad. And the thought that the whole process was kind of jammed up here, with Carmine and whatever suspended in the innermost, private-most part of Dad's private world . . . that would be a lot for him.

Dad stood there, anxiously awaiting an outcome. In the bathroom, Carmine took forever, waiting for the tank to refill, then flushing again. You know the way TV kidnappers clamp a hand over the victim's mouth to shut them up? Dad was doing that to himself. For as long as he could manage.

"Is everything all right in there?" Dad finally called when he could bear the wait no longer. He was also knocking at the bathroom door, as if Carmine could have simply forgotten to come out and just needed a reminder.

Finally, a heartier push on the handle, and I think the job was properly done.

It was like a surprise party, a parade for a returning war hero. When Carmine came out that door and saw us huddled around him, I thought he was going to run right back in. But before he had the chance, Dad took him literally under his wing. With a little excess of enthusiasm, he wrapped an arm around Carmine's slim shoulders and charged him through the remainder of the microtour.

"Here's the kitchen," he said, pulling him out of the kitchen. "These are the stairs. They used to have these stairs over there, but apparently a few years ago they moved them over here. I think that was a good move, don't you?"

Dad was gibbering; Carmine was spluttering out answers, half words, and grunts. And Walter and I were following, trying not to giggle.

Because we loved this bit of Dad. We loved all the bits, truly, but the bits of mad Dad were the best bits of all.

When he was good, he was good. But when he was not so good, he could be great. If some people thought he was a little nuts, we never minded, too much. We were happy, mostly. We were odd maybe, but we knew it, we dealt with it, and, at some level, we embraced it.

Upstairs, Carmine was treated to a lightning view of what Dad called "Dad's study" but we called more accurately the computer room since nobody studied anything in there and Dad was lucky to get any time in the room at all. In fact, he was far more likely to see the inside of his study because he was invited by me or Walter into a computer game than he was to be working on his own work. He really didn't enjoy doing his own work anyway, so really we were doing him a favor.

The tour wound up with a quick peek into Walter's neat, comfortable bedroom, all carpeted and gabled and warm, and an even quicker peek into mine.

"Oh god," Dad said, closing the door as quickly as he could, like there was a leaping lion on the other side.

He was exaggerating. The thing is, I find it personally offensive that girls are just naturally expected to be neater than boys. My bedroom is my statement.

"You're a pig, Sylvia," Walter said.

"No, I'm not, I'm a social commentator."

"Then you make filthy comments," he said.

By the time we got back to the door, Dad had excused himself, clearly bent on a mission involving the house, his notebook, and some mumbling. I myself thought we had come through our first house tour pretty well, for people who didn't do this sort of thing.

I loved the house more than ever. I loved its kinks and quirks and its us-ness.

And I was confident my bedroom had helped to finish off my little Carmine problem.

"So, still want to be my boyfriend?" I said to the visibly shaken boy who was standing in my doorway staring at his feet.

He looked up, first at Walter, then at me. He looked at me intensely, powerfully, like he was singing in a boy band.

"No," he said, high drama, "now I want to be your *husband*." He grabbed himself in a furious, celebratory hug.

I guess I had misunderstood the trembling.

He stood there hugging; Walter stood to the side of me laughing.

"Shut up, Walter," I said.

"I just thought of something funny, that's all."

"Did I hear somebody say *shut up*?" Dad called from someplace far, far away. I swear, sometimes he calls home from work, *sensing* that we have said something from his *never* list.

"How old are you, Carmine?" I asked as politely as I was ever probably going to be to him again.

"Almost eleven."

I shrugged. "Oh, now you see there, I'm already past fourteen, so that wouldn't work. But later on, when we're the same age, we'll talk about it again. Okay?"

He hugged himself so hard, he was unable to talk

until Walter went up and forcibly released him from his own grip.

"Pah," he gasped. Then started backing hastily away. "Wait till I tell everyone . . ." he said, and bounded away like a happy, demented jackrabbit.

When we had the door safely bolted, I turned to my brother, whose flickering, dancing smile expressed both hysterics and just a wee bit of apprehension.

"Do you suppose they're all like that around here?" I said. I noticed I had my hand on his arm in a very serious gesture, and we were standing close against the front door the way they do in horror films when a madman comes chopping his way in with an ax. I took a step farther into the house.

He was about to respond like a normal person, to sort of agree and to say something helpful and reassuring. Then he remembered to be Walter.

"What are you talking about? The only one acting weird was you. You could treat people better, Sylvia. And you better try a little harder before you get us all a reputation."

I stood, aghast, waiting for him to give, to laugh at his own absurdity.

But he held his pose of rotten seriousness.

"Hey," Dad called from the far tip of the house, "come here. Come, let me show you what the toilet's doing now."

"I have to go," Walter said, turning into the queen of England or something. "My father would like me to see what the toilet is doing."

And off he marched.

Right, I'd better be careful not to get the family a reputation.

The Brothers Grim

The thing about finches is, they can do an awful lot of chattering without ever telling you much about what's bothering them, or even if anything is bothering them at all. Their little songs are so cute, coming from their round little bodies and their serious little faces, that you always think everything is going okay, just from the sound.

They weren't brothers, of course, since they were married, but Walter and I decided to name them the Brothers Grim when we realized after the first several hours of staring at them that they were very grim characters indeed. If we got too close to the cage, the bigger one, Mr. Grim, would open his bright orange beak as wide as possible—which was a whole quarter-inch wide—and threaten us to keep a distance from Mrs. Grim. They were very much in love, the Brothers Grim.

So, with their habit of singing the same song come what may, tweeting and twittering away, you just might not notice if you forgot to fill the water dish for them one or two or three days straight when you were really busy with tests and life and things. You might not notice that, and they might not help things any by singing away and flapping away, much like they did any other day.

And it sounded just as beautiful. Just as beautiful, thrilling, sweet, and comical as all the other too few days they sang and filled our house before.

But their wee bodies couldn't take it. They couldn't go for very long, not the way a polar bear or an alligator could go very long between meals because they could store up great reserves of energy with their big meals and because they conserved their energy by not doing anything for anybody.

They couldn't go for very long without a bite or a drink, finches couldn't. Because they kept singing. Because they kept singing and kept burning it up, and who knew, what with all the business of life.

And so when he ran down, one Brother Grim just fell over and lay there among the tiny little seed shells all over his sandpaper floor, where I found him.

And it did not matter how much I cried and apologized and overfed and overwatered the other

brother, nothing was going to stop her from following along the next day and falling right down to that
same sandy, seedy cage floor.

And who could blame her?

It was awfully quiet then.

And the earth was still wet and soft and bald from
when we had buried the first one the day before, so
at least it was easy to get them back together. At
least there was that.

"Sorry, Sylvia," Walter said, patting the same
ground again with his bare hands. This was mostly
his job, the burying. We never quite arranged that,
but it became pretty much his job, and he took pride
in his job.

"Don't get your shirt dirty," I said.

"I won't," he said, and stood with his hands care-
fully extended away from his school clothes.

Dad had gone to work already.

"Wash up," I said. "We have to go."

Bygone

By the time he was done refiguring, the only part of the house Dad was still satisfied with was the outside.

We had the trees. We had the one cherry, and the two inedible apple brothers—crab and mutant. We had all manner of evergreen and leafy and baldy. We had the sea grass, the sandy soil paths, and the smell of the ocean everywhere you went, mixed all gorgeously with whatever mad plant life you happened to be standing next to. Even if the scent part did Dad less good than anyone, even if he had to work twice as hard as anyone, to grab hold of the scent part of things.

It was one of the saddest parts of my dad. It was one of the saddest parts, and on certain days—like especially on the most aromatic-breezy-oceansideharvesty days—I thought it may have been even the very saddest part of him, beyond even any of the old sadnesses. The fact that he couldn't smell things the way we could. Just didn't have it, because of, I don't know, an infection way back or something, he was never quite sure, or quite clear, other than that it just *went* on him. Left him flat.

He worked these days from the *memory* of scent, from before, from when he was younger, from before it left him. He was always a scent guy, he said, back before. It was his favorite sense, he said, back then.

"But we won't dwell on that now," he would always say, when he caught himself dwelling on it.

Anyway, it just didn't matter. What mattered was that he had to work a lot harder than you do or I did or Walter did to smell the apples in his own yard or the roses, for that matter.

I thought that was a horror. Especially for somebody who wanted so badly to smell the apples and the roses.

Then again, it might be the other way around. The fact that he had to make so much more effort—and you should have *seen* him, pressing a fruit or a flower so hard into his face and closing his eyes and squeezing and pulling the whole garden almost all the way into his lungs—that maybe if he still cared that hard, to do it that hard, that he appreciated it all the more than you did or I did or Walter did.

But, anyway, we had all that and more, all around us. We had the hedge that was our border, our moat, the spotty but more or less continuous twenty hodge-podge varieties of scrubby hedge. We had the big patches of grass, the wild wildflowers, the climbing ivies, the creeping border plants, the tough vines and thorns of our ruffian thistles and rosebushes.

And at the center of it, we had our fishies. A neat, odd irregular-shaped man-made pond sunk right in the middle of our overgrown secret jungle. Two fat contented lazy giant goldfish and one mustachioed black catfish squigged around in that pond as if they were putting on a slimy fashion show just for us, whenever we came by, any time of day. I named them Nina, Pinta, and Santa Maria after Columbus's boats he used to find the New World because this would sort of be our New World.

I wondered if they ever stopped for a rest, if they stopped for anything, if they did all that swimming just for us, or if they sensed us coming and snapped to it so they wouldn't lose their jobs.

Not that it mattered. It was enough that they were there, live and living like the rest of the garden, and the garden was ours.

You really would be happy to live here in these grounds, even if there were no house at the center at all.

So the outside passed inspection, even with Dad.

On the other hand . . .

Something happened. It happened to Dad, although if you asked him he would say it was the house, but something happened after the visit from Carmine.

It wasn't Carmine himself. Weird as he may be, he didn't actually do anything wrong. He just appeared, came into our new world. Walter and I tried to come up with the last time Dad had had anyone over.

"*Last* time?" Walter said. "What *last* time? Doesn't there have to be a first time before you can say a last time?"

Right.

While Dad was sleeping, if he was sleeping, things started creeping. Creeping up on him, getting into him.

And that is not what he likes at all. Things creeping in. He likes the outside outside. He started taking things very seriously. He started making big things out of little things, and some-things out of nothings.

"Did you see the color of it?" Dad asked over breakfast the next morning. He was at the table already when we came down, and his list—his dense, multipage list—was in one hand, a cup of Earl Grey was in the other. I smelled his tea before I was even down the stairs. Earl Grey is one of the finest scents, and it will pull you right up out of bed even on a Saturday.

"The bathwater, I mean. Don't be polite—you can't deny that you've noticed it. The gray bathwater, like somebody is blowing smoke through it before it comes out of the spigot. The water that looks like it's already been bathed in by some other family and then drained off to us. The *fish* bathe in nicer water than we do."

You couldn't miss it. Especially since the house didn't have a shower, and so we all took baths all the time.

"Um . . . did I notice? I don't think . . . Walter, did you notice any smoke water?"

"Smoke water? I didn't notice any smoke water. I didn't notice any *fish*. We have fish? Where are they? Can we eat them?"

He knew about the fish. And he knew about the bathwater. You couldn't miss it.

"Well, thanks, guys," Dad said, staring all the harder at his list, "but there's no way around it. We have to look at what we've got here."

Walter looked all around the kitchen. Then he looked at the pancakes, sausages, fruit, and juice waiting for us in the middle of the table, and he went to work on them.

"What, Dad?" I asked. "What have we got here?"

He took a deep breath as if he were about to go underwater for an extended period. Then he went for it.

"We have . . . rising damp coming up through the

floors. I found a mushroom growing up through floorboards in the hall closet. We have a cracked and rusted skylight in my study—"

Walter looked up from the food. "You have a study?"

"The computer room," I said.

Dad went on. "We have various minor roof leaks. We have this—" He stood up and pawed at the red-brown tile of the kitchen floor like a bull about to charge. "Look at this. It's like mud. It's like an adobe that never set. And the heating system. Have you noticed the heating system?"

"It's August, Dad," I reminded him.

"Yes, well, I noticed the heating system, because I have checked it. I turned it on, and then followed it around the house. And you know what? The radiators take turns. They don't all work at the same time. This one comes on and that one goes cold, then that one gets hot and that one turns off, and so on. How does that sound?"

I wanted to get as worked up as Dad, if only because I could never stand to see him get worked up all alone. But it was hard.

"It is August, Dad."

"It won't be August for long," he said with increased seriousness, as if he had uncovered some nefarious plot.

"Sounds to me," Walter said, chewing and talking

extra calmly, "like we just have clever radiators." He took another bite. "And lazy. Clever, lazy radiators. We'll call them claziators."

Dad just stared at him, until the dust of his words had settled.

"And loose window sashes. The wind will whip right through this place. I don't even think there is any insulation in these walls . . . and the walls. Didn't you think it suspicious how many of these rooms are papered, instead of painted? Huh?"

He was doing that *aha*, conspiracy-breaker voice of his.

"Well, no. I didn't actually think it was suspicious. But then, I never bought a house before. In truth, I didn't buy this one either. You did."

A quick flash crossed his features, like he was upset that I was insulting him or something. Then it went away again, lost in the tide of his home-improvement symptoms.

But the truth was, he did buy this house and all that went along with it. It was not shocking that Dad could possibly have purchased a place that wasn't exactly airtight, but so what? We knew he wasn't that kind of dad. We didn't *want* that kind of dad. Or that kind of house, for that matter.

Actually, this was the first house he ever bought by himself. He would have had somebody with him, when he bought the other one. Somebody would have been watching over his shoulder and seeing the things he just wouldn't see.

If there really was anything to see. And telling him to get a grip if there wasn't.

"Anyway, I have had a peek at these walls to see what is hiding under that wallpaper. Do you know what is hiding under that wallpaper?"

"Walls?" Walter said before I could stop him.

I gulped.

"Cor-rect," Dad said. "But only partly. Walls are what normal houses have under the wallpaper. This house has *weeping* walls. . . ."

He was very serious about this. I watched him go back and forth over his list, running one hand over and over through his thinning hair while holding his little notepad up in the air with the other one, like in the skull scene in *Hamlet*.

But I couldn't help it. All the things he said only caused me to feel more protective of the house, more involved with it. It was so not a boring house. It was The Diggers. And it wasn't anywhere near as needy as he was making it out to be.

"Stop picking on the house, Dad," I scolded.

"Picking, huh? Then there's the electrical system. Wait till I tell you what that does. And that old cat door—or should I call it the *rat* door . . ."

I motioned to Walter to pass me the pancakes. Then the maple syrup. He was already done with them, having munched his way all through the first half of Dad's rant. Now as I prepared to catch the second half, cabaret style, Walter was well fed and ready to jump in.

"Hey, Dad?"

"Yah, Walt?"

"Why did we move here again?"

For the first time since we had entered it that morning, the room went still. The air got heavy with the scents that were already there but that thickened now to fill the empty space—pork sausage, Earl Grey—scents Dad would have to breathe in twice as hard to appreciate like we did.

"Why?" he finally repeated after a surprisingly long wait. Then he waited a bit more, and when he came out of it, his answer fell limply out of his mouth. "My work," he said. "My job. We know that. We do. I moved for work."

As if he were convincing himself, and not doing a very good job of it.

I didn't like it. This was news to me, whatever it was, this was a sad surprise. We did move for his job, that was the truth. But every year they tried to get him to come to this office and only now had he decided to do it. There seemed to be so much more banking up inside Dad now. . . . I hadn't seen this. I hadn't known about this. And I am good—the best, even—at knowing about him.

"Dad?" I said. He could never hide from me. He could never fool me, if I didn't let him. "Why did we move here?"

He looked away, looked around, looked at food, at Walter, at his list, then at me.

"This and that," he drawled, "and that. Time, you know. Time. Really, kids, it was time for us to move. Away from there, from where we had been for so long, you know? Forever. Do you realize that, that you were there forever? For *your* forever, anyway? That's too much, I think, in one place. Time, really, it was time to go. Too much was back there, you know. We outgrew the old house, in a lot of ways. There was not enough space left in that old place. We crowded it out, that place, we grew up, and out, past its boundaries. Between us, and everything, there was just nothing left for us there. No room. It was all full up, like you know, like we all know, with old . . . *bygone* stuff. No room there. Time, it was, to get away from all the old . . . *bygone*. To start anew. Start again, afresh, anew. You know? You know."

Afresh. Anew. That would be starting again right there. *Afresh, anew?* A new language, practically, was what he was speaking. Dad did not speak *afresh, anew.*

"Afresh, anew, Dad?" Walter asked.

Dad nodded. He nodded sadly.

"Afresh, anew," he said.

It was all pretty foreign stuff to us, this new slant, Dad's full disclosure. But I think Walter and I were both ready to go for it. We probably knew—or I certainly should have—that leaving behind all the *bygone* stuff was no small part of our new look at life.

And it suited me just fine. I missed friends back home, missed my school, my old haunts and habits. But I didn't miss them so much that the idea of leaving didn't still feel like the overpoweringly right thing to do. Dad was right about it being time. And I for one was glad to hear him say it. That was one step ahead.

"But we won't dwell on all that now," added Dad.

And one step back again.

FitzWilliam

We probably never should have had a fox terrier. Maybe nobody should have one.

It was hard to tell whether he was a deranged genius of a dog or just deranged, but he clearly needed more than we ever gave him. Fitzy was always busy, always determined, always late for something. He ate raw carrots because they put up a good fight. He made a high-pitched whine-scream-laugh sound when he tried to get at something that was out of his reach but that he *had to, had to, had to* get at for reasons known only to himself.

On the rare occasions we troubled to take him in the car, he either stood up rigid, peering over the steering wheel like he was the driver, or he wriggled himself up into the raised back window area and peed, right where the driver couldn't help but see him in the rearview mirror. Neither of these things pleased the driver much.

FitzWilliam never slept that I was aware of. That may have been partly due to all the coffee and cola he drank as much as to his true nature. Because nobody could put down a Coke or a coffee anywhere within a mile of him. It was like he was bred to hunt caffeine instead of foxes. No place was safe—not the arm of a chair, not the hood of a car, not the highest shelf of a bookcase. He would scale a straight wall like a mountain goat to get a sip, and if Dad came into the kitchen one more morning to find him standing there with all four paws on the table while he straddled and drained a mug of Nescafé, he was going to do the little guy a serious mayhem.

Of course, that wasn't necessary. He was quite capable of doing himself all the necessary mayhem.

Just as he became capable of taking care of many of his own needs. Because we were not.

He played fetch with himself. He would take his spongy ball, bring it to me or Walter or once in a while Dad, and drop it at out feet. We would throw it. He would bring it back and drop it at our feet.

He would do this two hundred and fifty times. If you told him no, he would bark at you. If you sat down on the ground and tried to read a book or a magazine, he would place the ball on the exact sentence you were reading. If you tried to lie on your stomach and nap in the sun, he would stand on your back and drop the ball off the side of your face.

Only if he thought you had died would he go away and start on somebody else.

Eventually everybody died. We got good at pretending we were dead. Except Dad, who refused to play dead but would lock himself in the garage instead.

And when there was nobody left to satisfy him, FitzWilliam learned to do it himself. We thought it was funny at first, watching him take the ball with a running start, then let go so it was flying away ahead of him, as if somebody had thrown it for him. But we got tired of this, too, long before Fitzy ever did. He threw that ball. And brought it back and dropped it at his own feet. Then threw it again. And again. And again.

There was no end. There was no solution, no conclusion, no point. He just went at it until the sun set and he was hauled into the house, screaming, whining, barking.

He took it out on the house. He chewed the legs of chairs, the corners of carpets, a mahogany salt and pepper shaker set, and, one time, a lightbulb, which resulted in a mouth full of stitches and absolutely no decrease in enthusiasm or increase in sense.

So he stayed outside more. And more. He was left out unsupervised a lot until he started his collection of people's fresh laundry, then their gardening tools and whirligigs and hubcaps, and piled all the evidence up in a fairly conspicuous pile on our lawn.

He was tied up all the time after that, and he didn't like it. He would throw himself a ball, just far enough so he couldn't reach it, then strain and scream—with the ball two inches from his snout—for ages, pulling like he was going to drag the house along behind him, until somebody came and gave it to him. Then he went right back and did the same thing again.

Until it stopped. It was there, and FitzWilliam was there, and the air was full of the sound of him to the point where we could just about ignore him and just about forget why we got him in the first place and just about not think about where and why it had all gone wrong.

And it stopped, abruptly. Noticeably.

I was talking on the phone to one of my friends from school and felt this rush of *I gotta go*, and I told her I had to go, and I went.

And there he was, little FitzWilliam, when I got there to the yard where he was tied all the time. There he was, at the end of his tether, the ball he played with by himself all the time nowhere to be seen. There he was, with his back feet almost touching the ground, but not quite, hanging by the neck from the hedge he had jumped while chasing whatever it was that came into his yard and changed his day and maybe took his ball away.

He was detached, Fitz was, you would have to say so. He was fun, and he was lively. He would let you pick him up, let you play with him, wrestle him, cuddle him, whatever.

But he just let you. That was what I noticed. He just allowed you to do stuff, and then he would allow somebody else to do stuff, and really, he didn't care. He didn't warm to you.

He didn't love me, I realized. And I didn't love him. That was what happened, and the order in which it happened.

But FitzWilliam made me cry. And, for the first and only time, my father arranged a full pet-cemetery funeral for one of our pets. He paid probably enough for Fitzy's funeral to buy ten new Fitzys, even though we wouldn't even be buying one more.

He liked Fitz less than my other pets, Dad did. Truth be told, so did I, so did Walter.

It was about the saddest thing ever, the three of us standing there, dressed and proper, at the graveside on the day of FitzWilliam's burial. Nobody said anything. It was a gorgeous sunny day, the air smelled like honey, and nobody spoke a word.

The Beach at the End of the World

"Hi."

"Hi. Who is this?"

"Come on, stop teasing. This is Carmine."

Oh god.

"I wasn't teasing, Carmine. Did I give you my phone number, Carmine?"

Walter walked past the phone, giggling. I put my hand over the receiver.

"Stop laughing. Did you give him our phone number?"

"I don't even know our phone number yet."

"Carmine, where did you get this phone number? It's not even listed."

Here's the thing I realized about somebody like Carmine who flies a different sky from the rest of us:

you can never tell whether he is lying or fooling or honestly mistaken or just very, very lost.

"Um, somebody gave it to me," he said. "Somebody but I can't remember who."

"You know that's not at all believable, Carmine, don't you."

"No," he said in such a sad little way, like he was defending something dear to him, that I felt momentarily sorry. "I don't know that at all. I wouldn't lie to you, Sylvia."

I hated hearing him use my name. I didn't know why, didn't know what else he should call me. But I felt horribly intruded upon when he called me Sylvia.

"Don't call me that," I snapped, even though it was rude and unfair, and I knew it was unwise to yell at crazy people.

He sighed and snorted. "I have to say, you seem a little bit crazy to me."

Well. There was criticism to pay attention to.

"And another thing. If anybody lies, it's you. Remember that thing you said to me, about when I wind up as old as you?" He was building up a head of steam. "Won't happen. Did the math." Sounded very much like checkmate.

"Sorry, Carmine," was all I could think of to say.

"And don't call me that," he said.

Fine, I suppose I deserved that.

"What'll I call you then?"

"Barry."

"Right. Okay, Barry."

"I just remembered who gave me your number."

"Who?"

"Walter."

"Grrr. Whatever. What did you call me for?"

"I called to invite you to a party."

"Sorry, I can't go."

"I haven't even told you when it is yet."

"When?"

"Tonight."

"Can't."

"Why?"

"Busy."

"I don't think so."

"Don't you?"

"No, I don't."

"Why not? Why couldn't I be busy?"

"Because. You don't have any friends. You don't do anything, any of you. The three of you just stay holed up in The Diggers all the time. If you did anything, we'd know about it."

A wave of chilly goose bumps rolled over me, like a million cold tiny spiders running up the front of me, over me, and down the back.

"You little freak. What do you mean by that? And who are *we*?"

"Jeez," he said, and he sounded far away, apparently holding the phone at a distance. He was being dramatic—I wasn't that bad. "You know, Sylvia, you really are going to make me start thinking you're kind of crazy."

"I'm not crazy," I said crazily, because he was making me crazy, "*you're* crazy."

"I just meant," he said in that extracalm voice that nobody ever uses when they are really calm but everybody uses when they want to make you go berserk, "that people around the village, because you are new and because the place is so small, people tend to know what everyone's up to, that's all. Sheesh."

"Yah, well I live in this little village, and I don't know what anybody is up to."

"That's why you need to come to the party. So you can start finding out. It's a community, you know? You'll be a part of it."

Should that have sounded good? I didn't know. I suppose to a lot of people, especially people who had just picked up and moved to a whole new place, that would have sounded very good. Warm, even, comforting.

But I was guessing. It was pure guesswork, what other people might have thought, because all I could feel was what I could feel, and I felt shaken. Community. Community? Did I want that? Was that what we were here for? Small-town life? People looking out for each other? People looking *at* each other?

"Walter!" I called.

He came bounding up the stairs, and when he reached the cozy little landing between our bedrooms, I handed him the phone. "You lied about giving him the phone number."

"Um, possibly, yes."

"Why did you give him our phone number?"

"He traded me a bag of Reese's Pieces."

I shoved the phone into his hands before shutting myself off in my room.

Party. Ah, no, I don't think so.

"Of course we're going to the party," Walter said as he tramped behind me through the dunes. Dad, back at The Diggers, had sent us out on a mission to collect authentic decorative sea stuff for his new vision of the home. Probably instead of actually fixing and upgrading and rehabbing stuff he was going to spread around seashells and driftwood all over the place. Which was a finer idea altogether, in my opinion, and much more in line with Dad's notion of home-improvement work.

"Of course we are not," I said. I stopped and bent to pick up a pinkish something out of the sand. The body of a crab that had been eaten by a seagull sometime before I was born. I dropped it and moved on.

"You have to start listening, Sylvia. You never listen, you know that? You never listen, and you never think about other sides except yours."

"Because the other sides are wrong. And . . . what was the other thing?"

"You never listen."

"Yes, I do."

"No, you don't. You decide and you command and you insist, but you don't listen. Dad says you're not my sister, you're my *in*sister."

I got indignant. Then irritated. Then a little proud.

"I don't think he'd say that."

"Not when you could hear him. He's afraid of you like everybody else is."

Nobody is afraid of me—that is just ridiculous. He was really making me boil by saying so. Well, maybe not boil, but pretty warm. That is, smile. I took a quick dogleg down out of the dunes to make a run for the water, completely sure he would stay right at my heels.

"Hey," he shouted, right at my heels.

But the surf, as we got nearer, was working to smother all lesser sounds.

The first two waves, when we got as close as we dared, down over the gritty dry sand to the gritty packed wet stuff, *pounded* down when they broke like a team, *bam-bam*. It was that serious, emphatic type of surf day where the waves come in madly and then stop short. Followed immediately by the suck back to almost pure silence while the sea and we catch our breath for the next.

It was in these silent breaks Walter tried to fit his case.

"No joking, Sylvia, I think we should go to the party."

"Okay," I said, "why?" See, I could be reasonable and listen.

He started to speak, and the waves came, like my bodyguards.

Bam-swoosh-bam.

He tried again.

"It's a thing they do here, every summer, before school starts. Bonfire night. All the kids go. Nobody misses it. It's a tradition."

Now the waves came in, switching sides, to give Walter's words the impact. But not enough.

"That doesn't mean we have to go," I said coolly, picking up a piece of half-decent driftwood that was shaped almost like Nova Scotia. I knew my dad would love that.

"Yes, it does," Walter said, a bold statement made so boldly it didn't matter that a whopper wave tried to stifle it. "Listen," he said, speeding up to seize the space of wave silence as well as my own. "I don't want to be a freak, okay? If everybody goes to this thing and we are invited to this thing and we have a chance to get to know people and things . . ." He was shouting now, defying the waves, defying them impressively, I had to admit. "What's the harm? If we don't go, that's a bad start. We can be a lot of things, but *geek* sticks, you know, *weanie* sticks, *creep* sticks . . . I don't want to be any of those. We already have a hole to dig out of anyway, with the Gravedigger's Cottage situation making us look like hermit ghouls, so I don't think we should make it any harder for ourselves."

He was overstating things, as he does. We were fine. There was nothing wrong with the way we did things, and if Walter was suddenly seeing things in a different light—a *dim*, unenlightening light—then that was his problem. It was important that I not encourage him, especially on such a silly issue.

I walked on, and picked up the most wonderful dead starfish that had washed up on the sand. It was a beauty, stiff but still orangish, and as big as my hand. Immediately, I brought it right up to my face and breathed it deep.

I don't know if it is a guilty pleasure or not, but I do know it is a pleasure. I have always held a deep, passionate affection for the smell of old starfish, even rotting starfish. I do not know what it is about them, but they have always called to me, like a siren song— or a siren scent, I suppose—from the sea. And as I stood there with the starfish, smelling it, feeling the oddly rough clingy pebbly texture of its back and its uncountable sucky finger things, I closed my eyes and smelled the smell, felt the beginning mist coming down from the sky and the rising spray coming up from the surf, washing lightly over my face. A seagull flew close by and let out a little scream, and I could not imagine much of a better moment all over. I could not.

I opened my eyes again, and cast my gaze well on down the beach. It was an amazing beach, known locally as the Beach at the End of the World because you couldn't actually see the finish of it in either direction due to the curving-away rocky edges of the land, the frequency and intensity of the mists, and, well, the huge endlessness of it. We heard all this from the real estate agent when she was busy not telling us about weeping walls and Gravediggers. Couldn't blame her, I suppose.

I looked, I smelled, I felt it on my face, in my mouth and eyes. You could pretty well deal with anything else if you had all this. And it sure would help things if we could bring as much of this perfect outdoors as possible into our indoors.

My dad was going to love my starfish. He had a net, like a small fisherman's net, that he was keeping in the garage, and he liked to attach some of these sea-based things to it, like a sort of organic tapestry he was creating. I knew my starfish was going to wind up entwined there, and I hoped it would all wind up on some wall in the house, any wall in the house.

"Hey," Walter said in my ear.

I had my eyes closed again. I kept them that way. "Hey what?"

"Hey, it's starting to rain."

"That's not rain, it's mist."

"Still. Don't you think we should get going?"

I gave him a blind shrug. I liked the feels, the smells, the sounds of right here right now. Where does it say a person has to go in out of the rain? What is so wrong with rain?

"You should do what I'm doing, Walter. Then you'd enjoy it more."

He didn't say anything for a bit. Then he did.

"Are we all right, Sylvia?" he asked, altogether too seriously.

I opened my eyes. And there was his face.

It made me very sad, the way I was seeing it now. His round, round face with the round, round eyes, always seeming somehow to become even more perfectly circular when he got at all forlorn. The moisture in the air taking his longish caramel-colored hair and smoothing it down to frame all around that face. His heart-shaped little mouth, pursing and poking out just before he spoke.

"Don't you want to have friends, Sylvia?" he asked.

What kind of a question was that? Of course I wanted friends. I was very friendly. I loved having friends, and friends loved having me back. At the old place, at the old school, there was an actual waiting list to become my friend, because I just couldn't deal with the volume all at once.

I just didn't always feel exactly up to it. The effort of it. That was all. That would pass. Probably, sometime. Being friends and having friends would not always be so hard as it seemed now. Probably.

"You're my friend," I said.

He pinched and squinched his face all up, like he was exasperated with me. He could be a real little old man sometimes.

"Yes," he said, "I am."

"Good. Then that's settled. Let's go home and I'll make you and Dad and me hot chocolate."

He started walking ahead of me. He picked up a decent-sized piece of blue sea glass. He showed it to me. It wasn't completely worn the way the best sea glass should be—the edges were still kind of shiny and dangerous—but it was a beautiful cobalt blue and close enough for what you can find of sea glass anymore since people got all good and conservationist and insufficiently conscious of sea glass.

"I'm going to the bonfire," he said to me firmly, and turned to walk on.

Must have been the new house, the new situation,

making Walter McLuckie bolder and more adventurous than ever before. Maybe living in the Gravedigger's Cottage was making him feel like he had some kind of new powers.

Because this was a tall statement. For one thing, this bonfire—well after dark, without any adults present—was not even possibly the kind of thing Dad would say okay to. And that would mean doing it on the sly.

Walter McLuckie was never a sly guy.

And it would also mean doing it without me, because I wasn't doing it.

"Well, I'm not," I said.

"Fine," he said.

Not fine. Not fine at all.

Tank

Tank was the *I-dare-you-to-kill-this* indestructible pet gift I got from Dad.

It was a dare that should never have been made.

He was a sturdy tortoise, no doubt about that. He was stepped on a good many times, old Tank was, but he'd just suck himself up and wait for the danger to pass, then be on his way again. He ate greens— dark lettuce, spinach, broccoli, asparagus, snow peas, green beans. If they were a little bit wilted, he was okay with that. He had a particular fondness for green peppers which, if I chopped them up really small for him, he would eat with the gusto of a starved dog.

He ran for green peppers. He would smell them from his little nap area, which was a long pine box that once had a bottle of wine in it, and he would just bolt like a thoroughbred toward his bowl.

I may be exaggerating. I may, in the glow of hindsight, in the afterglow of Tank's afterlife, be making his achievements more notable than they actually may have been.

But he was great. He didn't gallop, maybe, but he really did charge after his green peppers. He was like a perfect child. Ate exactly the best things without a peep. Couldn't even make a peep if he wanted to, although he wasn't silent. I used to take him up and put him on me while I slumped extra far back on the couch in front of the TV. He would climb up my sweater, working so hard, his determined pointed beak pushing on up the mountain of me, then through the tangle of my hair, then around my neck as he searched for a better place to be. Then I would scoop him up, hold him to my ear, and listen to him.

The tiniest little breaths. *Huh-huh-huh*, he would go, right in my ear. Only audible if I had his head basically placed right inside my ear. *Huh-huh-huh*, Tank huffed. I never failed to giggle. I wanted to squeeze him so much, but we never could quite work that out, the proper squeeze.

Huh-huh-huh. Made the whole ocean sound in a conch shell seem like the honking of city traffic by comparison.

So he was quiet, and he was polite, he was no trouble and great company. He could go ages and ages without eating, he never drank except for what he could get from his veggies, and he never even tipped over and stranded himself on his back except when Walter did it just to watch. Even when that happened, I was the only one to get mad. Tank just kept on with his steady walking motion with his feet up in the air, as if he were still getting somewhere, until I turned him over and gave Walter a clap on one ear and an earful in the other ear that I can promise you hurt a lot worse. Yet Tank paid no mind, went on, on his way without ever trying to bite anybody, which would have been his right.

He was Tank, as we had hoped, but he was not indestructible. He seemed like nothing could bother him, nothing could ever get at him, but you find whenever you think that, you were wrong. You find that you had overlooked something. You find that you never really knew the whole story from the inside, and maybe you never can.

Because at some point something bothered Tank. He stopped eating. His food bowl sat there, and the vegetables went from crispy to soft, from soft to shrunk, from shrunk to decomposed. We cleaned the old stuff out and put in new crispy stuff that then also decomposed.

We let him roam around much of the time, like we did, but he got harder and harder to find. He would stay in closets, under furniture, behind the refrigerator. So many times I pulled Tank out of someplace and found him totally covered in dust bunnies, looking like some kind of very adorable mutant hybrid turtle kitten that got caught in the dryer.

But he wouldn't eat. We tried everything. Warming him up. Cooling him down. Keeping him in his box more, letting him roam more. Bathing him. Walking him. He didn't even take the occasional nip of a blade of grass, which he loved to do on his walks through the yard.

He wouldn't eat. And we couldn't force him. Some creatures you can force-feed. Ever try and force a piece of lettuce into the mouth of somebody who can suck his whole head into his body?

All I could do was watch. He shriveled. You couldn't see him losing fat, because everything about Tank went on inside, in his shell, his house, his protection. Where nobody could see, where nobody could get to him. His protection and his fault, the same thing.

But his legs shriveled, his head looked smaller. He would be lost for days at a time, and when I found him he would have one less toenail, one less toe, one less foot. Months he lived without a bite. And other than the decaying away, you could swear that he was fine with everything. He wasn't bothered. You would swear it.

The last time I found him, I knew it was the last time. I picked him up and dusted him off and held him to my ear. He stretched his neck, put his head in my ear.

Huh-huh-huh, he said, like always.

This time I didn't giggle. This time, for the first time, I decided he was trying to talk to me. He was trying to tell me things.

He had always been trying to tell me things, I decided, but I couldn't hear his little voice. Like in *Horton Hears a Who*.

I would have figured it out. We would have worked it out. I would have heard him. I would have understood him.

We just ran out of time.

Everybody's Walls

I never, ever liked the nighttime, even at the best of times.

No kind of a night owl, me. Morning owl, which wouldn't be right, I suppose. Morning sparrow? Morning dove?

I would like to be a morning cardinal, if I had my choice and if it didn't sound a little weird. They are the most beautiful birds, the brightest, most livid vivid birds, always visible, always *there*, always special. Never seen one alone, though, I don't think. Strictly in pairs.

Anyway, it's not about the birds—it's about everything else. I am suspicious about the nighttime, about the shadowiness of what and who is up and out there. Suspicious of what prefers not to be seen, which couldn't be a good sign—not wanting to be seen. There is just so much more hope in mornings, in the breaking light rather than the retreating kind.

I lay there in my bed, in the dark, when the August dark finally decided to arrive. I lay there listening. Smelling, breathing in the scents of the house and the sea, the scent of the darkness itself, which of course has its own odor. And listening, listening.

Stupid idea, stupid thing anyway. Bonfire night. No adults. Who needed it? It was dark, it was night. Bed was the place to be. You should always be in the place to be when it is time to be there. No place like bed.

The house whistled. Darned if Dad didn't turn out to be right about that. The house whistled when the wind blew.

Smash. Whoa. That was a tidal wave, practically, to sound like that all the way up here. That was a wave and a half.

He wouldn't go. He was too sensible for that, no matter how hard he wanted to seem otherwise. Walter had a good head on his shoulders despite it all. He was bluffing, to see what I would do; and now that it was clear I would do nothing, he would do the same. That's my boy, Walter.

Oh, no. I heard a muffled thump-thumping, like feet on the carpeting, and a rustling. In the hall right between my bedroom and Walter's. He was doing it. He was sneaking out. How could he? This was not like us. Not like me, not like him. This was not a McLuckie thing to do. Right—that was the point, he would say, not to do the McLuckie thing. Well, I didn't care for his point.

I got to my feet, scurried across the room in my nightdress, and threw the door open.

"Hi. Sorry. Did I wake you?" Dad said.

He was there in his summer pajamas, the ones that look like a short-sleeve button-down dress shirt and matching short pants with a hedgehog pattern stamped all over. He wore *everything* we ever gave him for Father's Day. Even gag gifts.

"No, Dad," I said. "I was awake."

"Oh, good," he said. "Do you smell it? It just won't go away. I think it's getting stronger, and just now it was distracting me so much I couldn't get to sleep."

Dad was like me, not liking the night much. He turned in when we did nearly every night. As he stood there in his shorty pj's, hunched over in sniffing posture under the mellow, bare forty-watt bulb dangling in the hallway, it made perfect sense he should be turning in as early as Walter and me. Or earlier.

"I'm not sure I do smell it, Dad." I gave an obvious sniff to the air. I shrugged.

"Sure you do. We talked about it this afternoon. You must be just getting used to it. Which might not be a bad thing, since obviously it won't be waking you up at night. But as the head of the house responsible for such things, I can't ignore that some strong, powerful scent is penetrating all corners of our home without trying to get to the source of it. You remember the smell."

I did now. And it was true—the house had a unique kind of an odor—but I figured all houses had theirs. This one was a sort of smoky damp, like wet charcoal, and it really only seemed to compete with all the other local smells when it rained hard—which it was not now doing. But the fact that Dad could smell it at all was noteworthy. And the fact that he seemed able to smell it even before I was able to smell it, *that* was altogether peculiar.

"Right. I do remember now," I said. "Wet charcoal."

"Right," he said, relieved, smiling at me. "Barbecue sauce. Very sweet, and vinegar, tomato, and molasses."

Anyway.

"But, Dad, do you really have to be hunting for it right now? Shouldn't you just leave it until morning?"

He pointed at me like I had a clever and original thought, which is what he tended to do whenever I gently told him what to do.

"Yes," he said. "I wouldn't want to wake your brother at any rate, would I?"

"Certainly not," I said.

He came to my door, grabbed my chin between index

finger and thumb, and kissed me on the tip of my nose.

"Night, Vee," he whispered.

"Night, D," I said.

I heard Dad's door shut downstairs just as I had gotten myself all tucked in and arranged, fluffed and settled in bed. Almost immediately, a feeling of rightness came over me; Dad in his place, Walter in his, the waves slapping more quietly in the distance, and the nighttime push of the late summer wind returning to an occasional gentle puff through the window screen. And as the feeling of right settled over, so, too, did the heaviness of sleep.

It seemed like one minute later I heard Walter's bedroom door close and his rapid little footsteps down the stairs and out.

I spent a good long time there, up in my bed, pretending. Pretending I didn't care. Pretending I thought he was just silly and that this was not my concern and that he could handle it himself. Pretending I was all cozy and snuggled down in my bed and sleep was there, right there, almost there, just about there, just about . . .

Pretending I was going to stay put and not go down to the beach after Walter.

Truth be told, it wasn't any good long time. It was maybe twelve seconds. I was up and dressed so quick, it was like my clothes had been standing there and I just jumped into them.

* * *

I didn't like it, didn't like it at all—the lonely dark night on the thin breezy road that took me the few hundred yards from our house to the beach. I got instantly a kind of new respect for Walter, the way he determined to do this, planned and waited, then got out here and made his way through the darkness to the unknown by himself, alone with nothing but his ten years and no me.

He was very brave, I thought.

He was going to need it, because I was going to kill him.

If I got there. I found this walk to be about the scariest walk I ever walked.

I didn't do this kind of thing. This kind of dark, late, lonely thing.

But I made it. And when I did, when I emerged off the road onto the sand dune wall that acted like a standing guard between the regular ordinary world and the beach world, I was yanked both ways with competing feelings of excitement and even more scaredy-catness.

It was, as advertised, a bonfire. A beautiful bonfire it was, too, once I allowed myself to settle down enough to appreciate it. It was tall, neat, and tepee shaped. Big fat sparks and embers shot straight up, like an upside-down funnel, in a perfectly orderly procession of light into the sky. Harmless and glorious and controlled all at once, as if every element knew exactly what it was supposed to do and we were not at the mercy of the chanciness of fire.

I stood there at the top of the dune, gaping like a total yokel.

And if that were not enough, there was a reception as if they had all been expecting me.

"Sylvia!" called one tall blond girl, hopping up off a log and waving at me with a big sweeping side-to-side motion like she was trying to signal a passing ship. She came running toward me then, and if she didn't have such a warm and welcoming tone in her voice I would have run in the other direction. I considered it all the same.

"Hi," she said, all breathless from scaling the dune. I suppose I could have met her partway instead of planting myself like a lighthouse. But I didn't. "I'm Jennifer."

"Hi," I said. "I'm Sylvia, which, I know, you already know."

"I know," Jennifer said. She tipped her head sideways, shyly. She had rounded pink cheeks, and even with just a good moon for light I could see she was blushing. Also, up close, her voice receded to a sweet, whispery trill. "You want to come down to the fire?"

"Well," I said, like I was being coy or something. Duh, maybe I could pass it off like I was just out for a stroll, walking a nonexistent dog or something. "Sure, I guess." Right, *sure* and *guess* contradict each other. But they fairly represented my feelings.

We walked through the sand, toward the impressive snapping light of the fire. Jennifer was barefoot, and as my sneakers had started filling with granules I pulled them off. When we reached the fire, I was surprised to realize that the whole party was a rather intimate group actually.

"Everybody, Sylvia's here," Jennifer said.

"Hi, Sylvia," everybody said.

Everybody but one, that is.

"Hello, Walter," I said firmly. I don't know what I thought I was getting at since he had only done exactly what he'd told me he was going to do. And since I never even told him not to do it.

Still. He knew what he did. So I fixed him with a you-know-what-you-did stare.

"Hiya," Carmine said. He hopped to his feet and came right up to me. I flinched, took a half step back. He was, of course, hugging himself furiously as he walked.

Jennifer put out a traffic cop hand. "Down, boy," she said, "and stop hugging yourself. What did Mom tell you about that?" Then for good measure she gave him a helpful little shove back toward his seat.

"Don't mind my brother," Jennifer said. "He's just confused because sometimes he thinks he's human."

"Ah," I said, thinking I liked having her between me and Carmine.

In addition, there were three other girls sitting around the fire, to whom I was introduced. There was Robin, a small black-haired girl with grinning eyes who played the flute—and played it beautifully—during most of the first ten minutes I tried to talk to her. Emma, who struck me as being most like me, fair to dark hair, medium height, medium shape, medium, medium, medium . . .

"I know," she said when I mentioned it. "In a way it's good, right? Like you always have a way to measure the world. Like everyone you meet, if they are taller than you, they are tall. If they are shorter than you, they are short. It's nice if you want to kind of blend in, but not if you want to stand out. I think, sometimes, that I am the very exact center of everything everywhere in the universe, like the hub of the wheel of everything. Don't you feel like that?"

Oh. Oh jeez. Well, no. Not really. Not actually. Not *ever*, as a matter of fact. Oh boy, I never even considered it, being the hub of the wheel of everything. How horrifying would that be?

"God, I hope not," I said, sounding I'm sure a little bit desperate.

But I was soothed quickly enough by the rising volume of Robin's flute competing with the elements, filling the swirling air with "Greensleeves."

And the last was Debbie, who I wanted to pick up and squeeze from the minute I saw her. She was littler than me by a good bit. She was smiley, almost in a perpetual state of laughter, though on closer look I could see that was just the way her face was built—eyes creased and ready, nose twitchy, mouth turned up.

But she was smiling, too. "Really glad you decided to come, Sylvia," Debbie said, first shaking my hand like this was a business meeting, then putting both hands on my shoulders like she was imparting sage wisdom—from a half foot below. "Walter said you were being kind of shy about the party thing, but here you are."

Right. Here I are. At the party thing.

You'd have to say it was more thing than party.

I saw no sign of anyone beyond these four girls, huggy-buggy Carmine, and Walter. This was supposed to be some kind of annual summer-ending tradition featuring the entire under-twenty population of the village. Was this the entire under-twenty population of the village?

"Where's the rest of the village?" I asked casually.

The girls exchanged glances. Walter just looked at me kind of sheepishly while Carmine looked at the ground like a bad dog.

"It's over that way," Debbie said, smiling and pointing in the general direction of the rest of the village.

I didn't want to sound unpleasant, but I kind of

needed more. "Where are all the other village kids?"

Again looks went around the bonfire like the wave at a football game. Robin resumed playing the flute, some hoppy Irish-jiggy thing.

Again, Debbie smiled, and Debbie gestured. "Over that way, I guess," she said, indicating, again, the village.

"You seem confused," Jennifer said quite rightly. She took me by the arm and led me over to a nice spot in the sand, sculpted sort of like a beanbag chair, just close enough to the fire. As we got near, something snapped, a little explosion. I jumped, scared, excited.

"Yes," I said, catching a breath, "I'm confused. A little. I thought this was like some kind of ritual, like a big celebration with every kid in the town and all the teenagers . . ."

I could see by the flickering firelit expressions that I was way off and sounding stupider by the syllable. Then, all eyes turned to Carmine.

"What did you do?" Jennifer said.

Carmine didn't answer. Walter also looked peculiar, and guilty, but in a different way. A stupider way.

Jennifer turned back to me. "Sorry, Sylvia. We were having a little beach fire. We do that sometimes. Just us. So then my brother, Mr. Delirious, starts blah-blabbing about how he knows you guys and how he's been hanging out with you guys and even your dad is showing him around the place and everything . . ."

Rude it may have been, but I found it physically impossible to look at Jennifer anymore. I found it impossible to look at the other girls or the fire or the sea. I could see nothing in this world other than the top of Carmine's demented, rectangular head. I stared at him so hard, if I were a magnifying glass he'd already have a white-hot pinhole in his head.

"So," Jennifer went on, "like I said, sorry. For Carmine. He has reality problems. He should be made to wear a sign or something."

I looked at Walter then, and he at me. He shrugged. I shrugged. He just looked so forlorn, so young, so dumb. We were here now, so what could we do?

"Tell us all about yourself," Emma said, "tell us *all.*"

Well, I didn't want to do that. But like I said, I didn't really want to be rude either.

"There's nothing to tell, really. We lived in New Hampshire before we moved here, up near the Canadian border. Then our dad was asked to move for his job. Then we came here. And then, tonight, we came here."

I don't suppose I really thought that would be quite fleshed-out enough. I hoped, though.

Everybody waited. You know that thing when people can help you out of an uncomfortable moment in the conversation, or they can just let it hang there, floating in the air and picking up gas until it's like a blimp. . . .

"And she had a whole lot of pets that are dead now and buried all over the yard at our old house," said Walter, being so helpful I wanted to bury *him* in the yard.

"Shut up, Walter."

I thought it would just be a minor embarrassing moment, but it was apparently more.

Debbie, Emma, Jennifer, and Robin all looked quickly to each other, pointing and nodding as if I had just said the secret word or something.

"What?" I asked.

Robin started playing something sad and mournful on her flute.

"Nothing," Jennifer said. "It was just that, well, we didn't *know* that exactly about you but we *knew*, you know?"

"No, I don't know." I didn't mind sounding a little crisp with them now, since they were creeping me out. Or making me angry. They were weird. Or they were nosy. I wasn't sure what they were, but right now they were too much of it.

"Listen, stop," Debbie said, getting up and coming over to wedge herself between Jennifer and me. "You're scaring her."

"I'm not scared."

I was fairly seriously scared. I was right about the night. No good, the night, no good at all. Should have been in bed.

"We just figured, there was some sort of . . . sorry . . . death connection to you, that's all."

"Why?" I said, sliding away from Debbie through the sand.

She slid along after me. Robin's flute played louder, but the sea, the surf, got oddly flat and quiet.

"It's not you, Sylvia—don't worry. It's the house, that's all."

"That's all?" I said. "That's all? Don't worry? I think I will worry, maybe. What about the house? What about my dead pets?"

"It's just what happens," Debbie said. She turned to address her friends. "Remember Sarah? She was really nice, remember? It was the same with Sarah. And what was the name of that girl before? It seems like such a long time ago . . ."

"I'm going home," Walter said, and stood up straight and expressionless as a toy soldier.

"Don't," Carmine said. "Please, don't do that. Here, let's go down to the water and throw stuff in."

Walter was allowing himself to be towed toward the water's edge, but he kept looking back at me kind of hopelessly. Serves him right. I told him not to come. Or I meant to. Anyway, he should have known . . .

Well, who got us into this? I said to him telepathically because I was too stunned to say it normally.

"The house," Emma said with an almost irritated sigh, "just attracts people who have, sort of, histories of *death stuff* attached to them. Your pet cemetery is probably the answer. But the fact is, everybody who has ever lived in the Gravedigger's Cottage has been just dripping in it."

"We are not—"

"Is it just the three of you, then?" Emma asked sharply, sweetly, softly.

"Emma," Jennifer scolded.

"That's okay," I said. "Yes. It is just the three of us."

They waited again, the blimp growing almost visibly in front of us.

But that was fine. Let it grow.

Eventually, Robin lowered the flute from her lips. I already missed the sound of it.

"How come nobody ever sees your dad?" she asked.

"People see him," I said.

"We don't see him."

"He's a private person. He's been busy. There's a lot to do at the house before he goes back to work. He likes his privacy. He's going back to work tomorrow. There's still lots to do though."

"Hmm," Robin said. Then she started playing "Amazing Grace."

"He's the Digger now, you know," Emma blurted, shattering the song, shattering everything.

"He is nothing of the kind!" I shouted.

Debbie came right up to me, put her small arm around my shoulders. I wanted to pull away but I didn't. I didn't because I also wanted to feel the way an arm around my shoulders made me feel.

"She doesn't mean it like that, Sylvia," Debbie said.

"No, she doesn't," Jennifer said forcefully. It was an odd mix, her high breathy voice and a bossy manner, but she did it. "She just means that that's the tradition, that the new owner of the Gravedigger's Cottage becomes the new Digger, that's all."

Again, that's all. That's *all*? I was beginning to wonder what folks around here would consider worrisome.

"My father is no gravedigger, thank you. And we don't change like that just because we moved into a house."

"You don't move into The Diggers," Emma said, "it moves into you."

Oh, how much I hate the nighttime. That probably would not have bothered me in the nice light of daytime. Nothing would have been hiding in there, in the dark corners of that stupid, stupid statement, if the beautiful burning cleaning light of daytime were here to clear it all up. But this was nighttime and I was out here, on the beach by the fire under the bald weak moon, and that stupid, stupid statement got in me and thrashed all around inside.

"Well, that's just stupid," I said.

Emma stood up. "Are you calling me stupid?"

The whole point of how Walter and I wound up here on the Beach at the End of the World in the middle of the night was that we wanted to get along, not alienate people. That was the idea.

"Yes, I suppose I am calling you stupid. And now I'm getting my brother and going home."

I got to my feet and stormed toward the surf, pounding with each step, with each step of course making no sound in the sand so why bother pounding? I expected somebody to follow me, to try and make things better. Nobody followed me.

"Walter," I called into the darkness.

Almost instantly Walter appeared, almost too instantly, his round white face blossoming out of the black on black of the water under midnight sky. I caught my breath. "We're going," I said.

"Great," he said.

I took him by the hand and led him back up the beach.

"Wait. Don't," Carmine said, rushing along behind us. He sounded wounded, genuinely sad to see us go—which was a weird bit of nice in the middle of the weird load of weird.

We passed through the group of girls, past their

fire, which was dying down. Robin was back to playing softly, something like "Taps" actually, piping the
fire into the next life. Debbie merely said good-bye to
us in a nice enough way, while Emma predictably
said nothing.

Carmine was still chasing after us as we headed
up the sand dunes, where we were also caught up by
his sister.

She didn't say anything before grabbing me
lightly by the elbow. I turned, pulling my elbow back.

It was nearly the exact spot where she had first
greeted me. We could have been standing in the same
footprints. "Don't take it so hard," Jennifer said. "It's
just the way things are. You inherited all that goes
with the house. No big deal. Not your fault.
Nobody'll hold it against you."

"Hold *what* against me?" I snapped. "There is
nothing to hold. This is stupid. We haven't done anything. We haven't *become* anything. My father is
about the farthest thing from a Digger you could
possibly get. And our cottage is a perfectly lovely
place."

I felt an overwhelming desire to cry, as I listened
to my words. As I heard myself defend my dad and
my home. I felt an even more powerful desire not to,
not now.

"Yah," Carmine said from behind her.

She was about to say more. Then she stopped

herself. "Of course it is," she said. "And of course you are good folks. We all know that. Look, I'm sorry Emma got you all upset. And I am glad you came down. Thanks for coming down. We'll see you again. Maybe we can come by, maybe help you work on the walls or whatever."

"What about the walls?" I said. "I didn't say anything about the walls. Why should anything be wrong with the walls. They're great walls."

"Oh," she said, shrugging and backing down the dune. "Small village, you know. Everybody knows everybody's stuff. Everybody knows everything. What can you do?"

"My *walls*?" I called after her. "Everybody knows my walls? How can a village be *that* small?"

"It can," she said, with a weary kind of sigh as she started trotting back to her friends. "Especially if it's a village that has Carmine in it."

Carmine. If we really were the Gravediggers, the next person death was going to attach itself to was Carmine.

For once, Walter did the right thing before I had to.

I heard a thump behind me.

"Ouch," Carmine squealed.

"Stop telling people about our walls and stuff," Walter said flatly.

Then Jennifer turned and called one last thing, "To make it up to you, we can let you keep Carmine."

"Hey," said Carmine excitedly, "that seems fair."

I walked on, didn't turn around. "Stop hugging yourself, Carmine. We can't keep you. I can't have any more pets."

We had crested the dune and were headed back down the other side, to the street and home.

"You could stop being mean," Walter said finally. It then occurred to me that he had barely spoken during the entire beach *party*. Like he was traumatized by the whole thing and only reanimated now that we were headed home.

"I'm sorry, Carmine," I said. "But I have been having a hard time."

We all kept walking. I kept looking straight ahead. The only real sound was Carmine's suddenly accelerated breathing.

"If you are hugging yourself again, I do wish you would stop it," I said. Kindly.

"Sorry," Carmine said.

We hit the street in silence, walked the sad, dark road in silence. The moon, which had been our only reliable light throughout the evening, was no longer reliable, as it tucked in behind thickening clouds. I could feel moisture in the air, even more than when we were down close to the sea. My hair was starting to get kinky, which is the world's most reliable rain forecaster, and my clothes felt damp.

We were almost home, but, boy, did I wish I were

home. Boy, did I miss my home. Boy, did I wish I had not left my bed. God, did I wish I still didn't know anybody here.

We stood at the back gate for a minute, trying to make a polite job of telling Carmine to go home. We were not even letting him inside the magic perimeter of our grounds, which was not the friendliest thing to do, but enough was, after all, enough.

"What time is it?" I said as nonchalantly as I could.

I meant it as a hint, rather than a real question, but Carmine had a watch. A watch with a luminous dial.

"It's exactly twelve forty-one," he said cheerily.

"It is *not*," I said, pushing Carmine away even though I didn't mean to. This was by far the latest Walter or I had ever been out. It was the *only* time we had ever snuck out. I had no idea it was this late, and felt immediately all panicky and guilty.

"We have to go," I said, and pulled Walter. "We have to go, Carmine, and you have to go."

We left him there and hurried through the gate.

"Okay," Carmine said, seeming for all the world like twelve forty-one was just lunch break for him. "I'll call you tomorrow."

I turned to suggest that maybe he didn't need to, but he was already gone from sight.

Inside, we shut the door as quietly as possible.

Then we stood there, frozen in the kitchen, sensing.

The house didn't feel awake. There was none of the warmth, the scent, the vibration of a house with awakeness in it. It was like when you creep to the bathroom in the middle of the night and you creep back again, really hoping that your dad or whoever is going to call out and ask if everything is okay but he doesn't and you scurry double speed back under the covers. It felt like that.

Except off there in the distance, not far away but in a way far away, Dad's radio talked in those husky, hushed tones of the middle-of-the-night radio talk guy.

He slept with the radio on all night. Sometimes it was loud, sometimes it was tippy-tippy soft, but always it was there.

He said it talked him through. We still hadn't talked about *what* it talked him through. But it talked him through.

I was happy to hear it, happy to know he was in there, happy things were now, for the moment, in their right places and that we were in our right places.

Never should have gone out. Should have been in our right places all along. Got to stay put, when put is the place to stay. Meeting people was a luxury, parties are a luxury, and right now I just wanted the basic comforts, not luxuries. I had the people I needed right here.

"Go on," I said in a growl whisper to Walter as I steered him toward the stairs. "We'll talk about it tomorrow when Dad's at work."

"He's not the Digger," Walter whispered back, kind of shaky. He is especially no good when he's tired.

"Of course he's not."

"Is it you, then?"

"Nobody's the Digger," I snapped. "God, just go to bed, Walter."

Gumby

Gumby acted like he loved me. He was a green tree frog with a white underbelly, massive orange eyes, and orange hands that had like bitty balloons for fingertips.

He was like gum the way his body felt, the way it stretched and twisted and stuck to absolutely everything, even glass, even if you tossed him like a little beanbag at the outside of his vivarium.

That's what they called the kind of fish tank setup you made for creatures like reptiles and amphibians, a vivarium. I always loved that word. *Vivarium.* So full of hope, that word, so bursting with life, ripe and fertile and vivid with life.

But he didn't just stick to me, when he stuck to me. It was like he knew me. Like he knew and he understood, and that I was practically his mother.

He held on so tight, wrapping his sticky orange hands around my thumb and looking right up at me, looking up to me all the time, every single second while I held him. While he held me.

His beautiful froggy face was like a question, all the time.

He never once tried to get away from me when I went to pick him up. He would be hanging in his tree branch in his vivarium, the branch that I took so long hunting down because of its perfect length and thickness and whiteness and smoothness, the branch that I polished and polished until it was like marble. He hung onto that branch for most of his time in the vivarium, staring off with the most remarkable wide-eyed faraway face on him, thinking something. Thinking some amazing, simple, froggy something until I opened up the top and he came back from his faraway place and looked up into my mommy eyes.

And then he scooched. Up and up and to me, finally climbing up with his weird elongated sticky motion, onto my hand, to grab on and go wherever I wanted to take him while he held my thumb with his orange hands and stared up at me.

He looked like he loved me. He may well have loved me. Nobody could say different. He for sure trusted me.

"I'm sorry, Vee," Walter said, patting the palm-sized mound of earth over Gumby. Over the bits of

Gumby we were able to find, outside, where he was never supposed to be. Where I was never supposed to let him be, defenseless against whatever. Where he must have counted on me not to ever let him be without me.

I pictured him, not putting up a fight. I pictured him, seeing what was coming and squeezing up tight his big orange eyes.

Chaos, Said Dad

I woke to a scritchy-scratch-tearing sound. It was in the walls, under the floor. It was moving around under me. I couldn't stand it.

I had not had enough sleep. As I said, I was never a night person, so typically I was up early—we were all up early most days—but I had been out late.

Didn't even sound right to me when I said it. *I was out late.* Why would I ever be? Me? Sounded so foreign.

But I was and so I needed to sleep later, but I couldn't because of the scritchy-scratch-tearing sound.

Maybe sleepiness made me more freaked, but I freaked. I jumped up on my bed and stood there, looking all over the place for whatever odd little or not-so-little creature was scuttling around down there.

Walter just then came sailing into my room, ignoring my all-important closed door, running in and jumping up on my bed next to me.

But to be a guy, to do the manly boy thing, he had to be sure not to look like me. He couldn't catch himself doing what I was doing, which was basically the old cartoon lady-on-a-chair-eek-a-mouse routine. For while he was certainly right up there, shoulder to cowardly shoulder with me, he made out like it was something different.

He put his hands on his hips. More, he put his *fists* on his hips as he surveyed all around us and inquired nonchalantly, "So, what's going on down there, huh?"

My hero.

"I don't know what it is, Walter. If I knew what it was, would I be standing on the bed like a big chicken, like you?"

"I am not a big chicken. I came here to check on you."

"That's nice," I said. "You're a very thorough checker."

Meanwhile, the sound went on. It was right under us now, louder, insistent, but definitely not in the room with us. It was just after nine, and Dad would have left for work already, so the world as we knew it was without its legs just then. Things could go bump in the night—or scritchy-scratch in the daytime, even—but if we knew that patrolling down below us was Dad, we could deal.

But now he was gone.

And we were alone.

In the Gravedigger's Cottage. With the Sound.

"*Why* did you make us go to that stupid bonfire last night?" I said, slapping Walter on the arm. "This is all your fault, making everything seem so spooky."

"What is all my fault?" he asked, giving me a shove that sent me backing into the headboard.

I was about to give him a good sharp crack on the shoulder when suddenly the scritchy-scratching stopped.

We stood there, listening to the house.

"Hey," the house called, from downstairs.

It wasn't the house, of course, it was Dad. But it was almost as alarming. Dad was supposed to be at work, first day back after vacation, first day back after moving. First day at the new office, the new everything.

Walter and I tumbled off the bed and down the stairs, where we found Dad in a pair of white house-painter overalls, which I didn't even know he had, cut off for shorts. He was standing at the far wall of the living room, two distinct expressions on his face at once, both grimly determined and satisfied. Like one of those people whose mouths curve downward when they smile, even though he was not one of those people. Around his feet were several big uneven shreds of old wallpaper he had just torn down. He held a putty knife up in front of him like it was the focus of his show-and-tell.

"Good morning," he said.

Walter said a quick hello, then went right over to that wall. Within three seconds he had uncovered a vulnerable loose corner of wallpaper and was energetically separating it from the wall with that old familiar scratching noise for background.

"Good morning, Dad," I said, remaining right where I had landed at the foot of the stairs. "We were wondering what that noise was. I was afraid it was some kind of critter loose in the house."

Dad turned his back to me, put his hands on his hips as he looked the half-bald wall up and down. "Nah, it was just me," he said. "Though turns out we do have a rat around."

"No!" I shouted and started walking fast-motion backward up the stairs. As if rats couldn't climb stairs. Walter paid no mind, because he was completely wrapped up in the boy joy of tearing something down and leaving it right there on the floor without being in trouble for it.

"It's not in here, Sylvia, don't worry," Dad said. "I've only caught glimpses of him here and there creeping around the grounds."

Don't worry. Does anybody ever stop worrying

when somebody tells her to? I'd rather have a dragon "creeping around the grounds" than a rat.

"Why are you here, Dad?" I asked, cautiously descending the stairs again.

He turned, caught off guard.

"Why aren't you at work, Dad? You were supposed to start back at work today."

He shook his head, then went to nodding and smiling reassuringly. "Couldn't do that," he said, as if he was explaining the most obvious thing in the world. "Couldn't leave you guys here alone . . ."

If it had been my dad's mission to be as surprising as possible this morning, then he was doing a top job of it. Because, wonderful and protective though he was, he was not normally against leaving me and Walter in the house by ourselves. Nor should he have been. We were very responsible people, had learned long ago not to stick our fingers in light sockets, not to chew razor blades, not to communicate in any way with salesmen. I would go as far, in fact, as to say there were times, many times, when a popular vote would conclude that I was clearly the most mature person in this house; and even if the scales were tipped in my favor by the other two contestants being gender handicapped, that still didn't make it any less the truth.

So, his explanation for being home didn't wash. Even Walter knew it.

Walter stopped tearing up the wall. "Dad? What does that mean—you're *never* going to leave us alone ever again?"

Yikes. Much as anybody loves their dad, that's got to be a little scary.

"No, of course it doesn't mean that. I just realized that the house needed more, considerably more attention before I could feel comfortable going back to work. The house needs me. The walls, the chimneys, the plumbing . . . here, feel this bit of wall, and you'll feel it weeping."

I had to butt in. "Of course they're weeping. I'd be weeping, too. You never stop picking at them like a scab, Dad."

He turned from the wall and gave me a brave smile. "Thank you, honey, but I'm afraid it's chaos."

I felt myself glancing quickly this way and that over everything.

"It's not, really, Dad."

"Chaos," he said again, not disagreeably.

It was weird, but the idea of its being chaos seemed to provide him some level of satisfaction.

Or maybe not the chaos itself, but his *war* with the chaos.

"You're not going back to work?" I asked gently.

He smiled, like he had a great surprise for me.

"Just a little leave of absence," he said, "until everything is in order here. I've earned it anyway.

Not a sick day since back before you guys were in day care."

He turned back to the wall and started making a rather weak assault on the more stubborn bits of paper with his little putty knife. He was never any kind of do-it-yourself guy. In fact, whenever the phrase even came up on TV in a commercial or in some stupid show, he would instantly reply to whoever said it, "No, buddy, *you* do it *your*self."

"Could you fix me a cup of coffee, sweetheart?" he asked as he chipped away at the wall. "Light, four sugars."

He said it was what made him such a sweet man, the extrasweet coffees. I said it was what made him a little hyper. But at least it was helping to rid us of that horrid wallpaper that suddenly looked like it had been stitched together from rotten banana peels.

Hard on the eyes, yes. But chaos?

Hyper, though, was the way everything started to feel. We went from a nice slow summertime thing, hidden within our green garden walling, listening to the sea from a friendly distance, to a situation too fast, too uncertain, too busy.

"All right now, what do you think?" I said to Walter once we were out of the house. After breakfast Dad gave us a grocery list and sent us out while he plowed away at critical home improvements that only a few days earlier were not so critical.

"I think I hate grocery shopping. I think I wish I could have stayed back there and wrecked the house with Dad."

"That's not what I was asking about. I mean about the bigger things. I mean, what do you think about Dad staying home and about all that creepy gravedigger stuff last night at the beach?"

We were turning the corner at the end of our road, coming in sight of Beachcomber, the local supermarket that was no supermarket but more a cross between a Store 24, which was not open nearly that much so should have been Store 8 or Store 5, and a teeny-tiny Walgreen's, selling beach pails and Styrofoam surfboards and cheap cassettes.

One of the keys to being Walter was his superhuman ability to not see what he did not want to see, and to see what he did see in precisely the way he chose to see it. This skill got Walter through— through all the big things that happened in life and the small. He was great at it, and I had to admit that much of the time I envied him because it seemed to work so well for him and because I could never manage it. I admired it. I loathed it. Here Walter summoned up all his powers of denial.

"I love having Dad around," he said as if he were accusing me of disloyalty or something that stupid.

"I wish he stayed home all the time. And I don't know what was so weird about last night."

"Hi, guys," Carmine said, popping out from a bush or a manhole or a puff of smoke somewhere. A perfect visual aid to accompany my discussion of weirdness.

"Sure you don't," I said.

"Hi, Carmine," Walter said, as if I hadn't just spoken to him.

"Hi, Sylvia," Carmine said, as if Walter hadn't just spoken to him.

"Yah, hi, Carmine," I said. "*Don't* hug yourself or I'll scream."

It was an odd pose, Carmine frozen in midflail, but he managed restraint.

"Hey, that was fun last night, huh?"

"'Huh?' is right," I said. "What fun? You mean the part where those girls scared the wits out of us with spooky stories about our house? In the middle of the night? Fun for whom?"

"I wasn't scared," Walter said.

I threw him a look but did not bother speaking. We continued walking along to the store, hauling Carmine like a barnacle stuck onto our hull.

"I guess you're coming shopping," I said as we stood in the beam of the automatic door sensor. The door opened, tried to close, opened again, tried to close. It seemed to be getting angry at us.

"Well, sure, if you want me to," Carmine said.

"Cool," Walter said.

"Cool," Carmine said.

"Cool," I said, entering third and lonely with my wasted sarcasm.

"Now listen," Carmine said, trying with all his heart to be some kind of leader for us, "I'll show you around. I know this place very well. I know everybody who works at Beachcomber, and they all know me."

"Look," said the tanned and tall girl working the one register, "look who it is."

It was hard to tell who she was talking to since we couldn't see anybody else here but ourselves. And we knew who we were, pretty much.

She grabbed the snake-neck microphone, "Shirley," she announced to somebody out there, "the kids from The Diggers are here."

We were known. We were known and we had a title, *The Kids from the Diggers*, and it was announced over a snake-neck microphone, which basically makes a thing official. The phrase *Eee Gads* actually came into my head for the first time in my life. It was an *Eee Gads* moment.

Shirley, who looked like she was the other girl's mother, came out of the back room from behind the deli counter. She was eating a sandwich but managed a big friendly wave and called, "Hi, kids. How you getting along, okay? That pest Carmine bothering you?"

"See," Carmine said with no small pride. "I told you I know everybody."

"*Everybody* knows everybody," I said.

"Yes, you're right, it's great."

"I didn't say that, I didn't say that at all. It makes me nervous, to tell you the truth."

Walter grabbed the list out of my hand and started pushing a cart down the first of four aisles.

"First thing," whispered Carmine, "you have to be careful with the fruit here. The fruit can taste like meat, if you know what I mean."

"I don't know what you mean—I never know what you mean," I said. I walked ahead and grabbed the first bag of oranges I could reach and threw it into the cart, to show him I would be just as reckless with the fruit selection as I wanted to be.

"There are no oranges on the list, Sylvia," Walter said.

"What? Why not? What?"

They were only oranges, right? But we always got oranges. We liked doing things the way we always did them, me and Walter, and we always got oranges. We liked things consistent.

"We always get oranges. Why are they not on the list?"

"They just aren't. There are—oh wait, there are

oranges. But he wants canned mandarin slices."

"Canned?" I stared at Walter. Then I stared at Carmine, who was poised to give the inside story on canned mandarins. "Don't say anything."

"Yup. And canned peaches. As a matter of fact, there are lots of canned things. Vegetables, fish, Spam—"

"Spam? *Spam?*" I snagged the list. "Deviled ham, chicken spread, corned beef hash, Kool-Aid, Coffeemate, powdered milk, instant mashed potatoes . . . Pop-Tarts . . ."

"Don't you guys have a refrigerator?" Carmine asked. "'Cause if you don't have a fridge, I know a guy in the village—"

"It's like he's planning for a snowstorm," Walter noted. "I love it when we get all packed in and prepared for getting snowed in."

I was forced to burst his sad little bubble. "Walter, *August.* It's August. It's not going to snow. It's not going to snow for a very, very long time. Why is Dad preparing for some emergency we don't know about? Powdered milk. I don't want to drink powdered milk. Neither does Dad."

"Oh, it's not so bad. Especially if you mix it with strawberry Nestlé's Quik. We have to hang together through these things, Sylvia. As long as we all pitch in together—"

"Through *what* things? There are no things. And I

don't feel like pitching together—"

"I'll pitch together," Carmine said. "Can I pitch together with you? Sounds like fun."

"It is fun," Walter said.

"No," I snapped, and started zipping up and down the aisles, filling Dad's request for every nasty disgusting army surplus food item they had, but grabbing as well several items that actually had expiration dates that I might live to see.

The bags were, as you might imagine, very heavy. Half of the weight must have come from the packaging alone, and Walter no longer thought Dad's disaster menu was so amusing. I was glad enough to have Carmine for help at that point, but by the time we reached our back gate, I was ready to dismiss him.

"Well, thanks," I said in a heavy-hint kind of way.

Carmine smiled broadly and said I was quite welcome as he brushed right past me and on up to the house.

"Why do we have all this survival food, Dad?" I asked as I plunked my bundles on the kitchen table. Walter followed, dumping his bags, then Carmine did likewise.

"Hi, Mr. McLuckie," Carmine said.

Dad looked for a moment like he didn't know who Carmine was. For a moment I wasn't sure I knew who this dad was either, covered in some kind of white plaster dust head to foot.

"Hi," he said to Carmine. Then, more friendly, more familiar, "Oh, right, hi. How's it going?"

"It's going great," Carmine said. "Can I help you with some of this work? You look all . . . dusty. Like you could use some help. I can help. I like helping. I like this house."

He was definitely freaking Dad out now. Dad took tiny little steps backward from Carmine, like he was looking to bolt.

Good. It was about time somebody else got the creeps over the kid.

"Yah, Dad, he can help," Walter said. "Let us help."

Dad started looking around, still looking like he was searching for an oversized mouse hole to shoot through. But then I realized he was looking at his handiwork. At his do-it-himselfing, trying to see what he could share with two ten-year-olds.

Any of it, from what I could tell. Because it looked like it was already being done by ten-year-olds.

He had left the wallpaper stripping in midstrip. As if following the line of his eye and driven by a very short span of attention, he followed the dead paper down off the wall, onto the floor, where he encountered a floorboard that somehow did not meet his approval. The board, pried up apparently with that same single trusty putty knife, lay at Dad's feet. The boys ran to it and stared down.

"Cool," Walter said.

"You get to see right down into the cellar," Carmine said. "You are so lucky."

"Dad?" I said as the three of them stared down into the hole like it was all the mysteries of the universe explained and not a hole in our floor.

Dad looked up at me. He smiled. He shrugged. He turned and led the boys through the far door into the hallway.

"Why did you have to pull up that floorboard, Dad?" I said as I joined the team at the front door.

"The smell," Dad said absently. "I caught the odor, that odor. And you know, if *I* could smell it, it had to be serious. I had to trace it."

"Did—"

"Didn't, I'm afraid. It wafted away. Now. Three windows anyway, the three on this side of the house, front room, kitchen, and bathroom, all are going to need to be replaced. And probably this door . . ." He walked through the lovely glass-paned door into the little foyer that led to the outside front door. It was an okay door. Not a great door, not a bad door. A door that wouldn't offend anybody. A door that you probably wouldn't replace. A door you certainly wouldn't skip work over.

"Very drafty. Rotting. Woodworm, I suspect," Dad said with great authority that came from god knows where. "It's chaos," he said again.

"Right," Walter chimed, tapping that same well of

male phantom knowledge, "woodworm . . . chaos . . ."

"I like that door just fine," I said, feeling already weird about defending a door.

"The house is not tight," Dad said, leading the way up the stairs toward what all he had found wrong with the upper level of our world. "It's not secure, it's not impenetrable to the elements, the way a house should be."

I stopped at the foot of the stairs, watched as he led the boys along, listened as he addressed the gaps and spaces and weaknesses of all that surrounded us. "Wait till you see all the chaos up here," Dad said.

I did not go along. I went back to the kitchen and started unloading all the indestructible provisions we had brought home to see us through whatever chaos was coming.

Ever Anymore

I remembered that my mom was afraid of germs. I remembered that she was afraid for herself but mostly for me. She was always protecting me from germs, keeping me out of drafts and away from people who coughed. I remembered that me and my mom spent all our time together, as if there were two people in the world for much of the time, and that those two people, me and her, were always warm and safe and together, bundled up and cozy and safe. I remembered that she didn't even like me to touch the mail, because somewhere out there somebody dirty may have licked it.

I did not remember my mom's funeral, because I did not go. I remembered one part of her wake because I was allowed to go. I remembered being brought in and the unusual smell, not good, not bad, but unusual—bakey, warm, and fruity—of the funeral parlor. I remembered the smell and how it made me feel upset and scared, but that I was with my dad's cousin Diane and she was leading me in by the hand, and so I could do it okay. I remembered that I was on my way up there, toward the casket where they were keeping my mom, where it was open and everyone could look at her and I knew she would not like that at all, but that everyone for the moment seemed to be looking at me anyway, while Diane led me by the hand. I could at least do that for my mom. I remembered it being long, like a mile from the front door to the casket, and it took forever.

I remembered hoping that people who were coming to see my mom were taking care not to breathe on her because she wouldn't like that.

I remembered hearing kind whispers of people all the way up that mile aisle as I made it almost all the way to making it all the way to my mom when I saw my dad.

I remembered stopping, planting myself right there in the middle of that aisle like I was vines growing up out of the floor, when I saw my dad. When I saw my dad crying out his heart, crying out his guts, crying out of his mind up there next to that casket. My dad. I remembered he did not even know I was there.

Ten cousin Dianes would not have been strong

enough to get me any closer to that casket, to that mom, to that dad.

I pulled with all I had, and if I had to put Diane over my shoulder to get out of there I would have. But I didn't need to. She took me out, took me home, stayed with me, tried to stay with me. She tried to hold me, tried to comfort me, tried to touch me, and in the end just about managed to follow me around room to room, chair to bed to yard, following, watching, talking, hovering, until finally I was finished, it was all out, I had nothing left, and I curled up on my parents' bedroom floor and fell asleep.

I remembered not to use the word *parents* anymore. Ever anymore.

Leakage

I started to worry.

"Vee, play soccer with me," Walter yelled from the backyard.

I was on my bed, reading, with my bed dragged right over to the open window to catch the sweet summer sea breeze just letting itself in. I was relaxed, lost in my book that was also about the quietness of summer and the sadness of it ending. I loved reading about sadnesses.

"Come on," he said again, his manly, iron little voice coming through the window and interfering with my mood and the breeze and everything. "Please, Vee."

This was not good. Not right and not good. This was not my job. Soccer was not my job. Dad was supposed to play soccer in the yard, he always did that, and if I wished to interrupt my book or my music or my just doing nothing because what they were doing wound up sounding pretty good, then I would do that; and usually, they made it sound good enough that I didn't want to be left out and so there I was. But I was not the first option.

I went to the window.

He was right down below, his brilliant white soccer ball—he washed it more often than he washed himself—squeezed tight in his hands. He looked tiny down there, all washed out and shrunk in the brilliant sunlight and the sandy ground.

"Play with me," Walter said.

"That's not my job," I said.

He just stared up at me.

"Dad is supposed to do this stuff, Walter, not me."

"He's doing other stuff."

"What stuff?"

He paused, bit his lips, as if what he had to say was unspeakably distasteful. "*Inside* stuff," he said.

I sighed.

It had been a week now since Dad had decided that the house was too porous and drafty, too insubstantial and insecure, too suspect, too open. In that time, he had started projects everywhere. Anyway, he started what he called projects, what you or I might call messes. Putting insulation in the attic. Weather stripping around any doors and windows he decided didn't need replacing and taking a fat red felt-tipped marker and drawing a giant X on the ones that did. He worked for hours one day inside the fireplace, making sure the chimney flue was completely capable of opening and, especially, closing. Though we had no idea how much he achieved, he came back out of there at the end of the day looking like a coal miner. Had to throw away his white cutoff bib overalls, so at least we achieved that.

He was always doing something, really *always* doing something, rarely finishing anything, before a new and more important crisis caught his eye and he attacked it. All of his concerns seemed pointless to me and totally unnecessary until I finally saw the thread of what he was pursuing and that he was truly striving to make the house 100 percent airtight, secure, hermetically sealable inside from outside.

Moving away from old life and death was not enough. He had to lock it out in case it tried to follow us.

"Ah, Dad," I said when I found him checking my own window sashes for rattles, spaces, breathability, "isn't *some* air *supposed* to get in?"

"You'll thank me, soon enough, when that ocean wind is banging on your window at night."

"That'll be me, banging on the window, because I am smothering to death."

He left my window alone. But I knew that wouldn't be the end of it.

Walter was still not as concerned about all this as I was, not as concerned as he should have been. Then one night the three of us unwound in front of a National Geographic special about the spread of urban and suburban wildlife. We all watched with what I thought was the usual fascination, until I noticed on passing the popcorn that Dad's expression was more what you would call horror. He skipped the popcorn, got himself up out of his old favorite chair, and went straight to the kitchen. He removed the famous cat flap with a hammer and his trusty putty knife in a frenzy of banging and pulling and grim speech making about how many different varieties of intruder could fit through that flap, if they hadn't already done so and were now taking up residence in the walls and basement.

He didn't even have a proper alternative to the cat flap worked out, and he gasped in terror at the new and improved *giant* gateway between the outside world and ours before quickly hammering Walter's regulation dartboard up as a stopgap.

I looked Walter. He looked at me. Right.

It took cat-flap fever to do it, but Walter appeared ready to help with the worrying.

"Come on down, Sylvia."

He looked so sad and helpless there, I had to go.

"Yah, you know what, Walter?" I said, taking the

ball out of his hands. "You only react to things when it costs you something."

"Not true." He grabbed the ball back and headed for the goal we had in the corner of the yard.

"It is so. You only started worrying about Dad going nuts when he nailed your dartboard to the kitchen door."

"It's *still* there," he said, incredulous at the unavailability of his toy more than at any of the possibly more substantial issues of our father's behavior. "He could have replaced it by now with something permanent."

"Right," I said. He rolled the ball toward me, and I stopped it by putting my foot on top of it. "There's that, and now you're only coming to me because you don't have him to play soccer with you."

"Not true," he said.

I kicked the ball at him ferociously.

He didn't even move. He waited for the ball to come rolling in and bump into him.

"He isn't finishing these things because he doesn't *do* these things, Walter. Don't you know that? Don't you know Dad? He isn't one of those hardware-store guys. He doesn't *do* things. He isn't a *doer*. He doesn't even like doers. He likes to sit in his chair. He likes to go to flea markets and maybe walk on the beach with us once in a while and go to stupid movies and play Parcheesi and backgammon. He likes soft socks, and he does not like overalls."

Walter kicked the ball back to me. I kicked it back to him. Then we did it again, never gaining any speed or force. It was like we were playing under water.

"Maybe he's just spreading out a little. Maybe he's trying out new hobbies."

"Spreading out? He spreads out from his bedroom to the kitchen to the basement, and that's about it. Hobbies? His fingernails are dirty, Walter. Have you seen those fingernails? When did he ever have dirty nails before? He doesn't like dirt. He likes baths, remember? He likes showers and baths, lots of them, and he likes his bathrobe. He doesn't like dirt and overalls and hammers. He doesn't like *hobbies*."

I decided enough was enough with this nonsense. I opted not to kick the ball from afar, and instead charged him with the ball, which I was always better at anyway. I ran in, shifted left, shifted right, went straight in at him.

And banged right into him, without ever getting a shot off. I bounced right off Walter's chest, went back in the direction I came from, then landed right on my backside.

I sat there looking up at him.

Walter's healthy, round, happy face, sometimes mean face, always *there* face, puckered and pulled in, collapsed on him as he stood looking down on me.

I felt my eyes go wide, my throat lump up when I saw. He didn't do this, didn't show it anyway, and certainly wouldn't do it over just bumping me to the ground.

He reached down with both hands and pulled me up, his face still all strangled up as he asked, "What's wrong with Dad, Vee? What's going to happen?"

When I stood, I was just about eye to eye with him. I figured it was only a matter of months before I was going to have to start looking up at him. But he still had a long way to go to really catch up.

"I don't know exactly," I said. "But I know it will be all right. Dad is Dad. He is always going to be Dad, no matter what. We didn't get all the way to here, from all the way away where we started, through all the everything we went through just to suddenly go poof. Right?"

He looked at me a little bit harder then, as if to see if it was, in fact, right. As if the answer to the rightness of all was to be found just a little deeper inside my eyes.

His face uncrunched. Not all the way, but enough to make my own stomach feel a little less filled with bowling balls and bees.

"Right," I said.

"The fish are all dead," he then said.

"What?"

"They're all dead. All three of them. They're gone.

Dad says the rat got them."

"God, not the rat again," I said as I spun away from Walter and headed for the goldfish pond. "He blames everything on the rat. The rat broke the garage windows, the rat stole the garden hose, the rat scratched his car, the rat's been making screeching noises outside the windows at night. Like, we don't have just a rat anymore, that's not enough, now we have to have a rat with a *grudge*. Have you even *seen* this rat, Walter?"

We were just approaching the pond.

"Yah, I think so," he said, stopping me dead.

"You have?" I said, turning on him.

"Yah. Maybe. I think so. It was at night. You were in the bath. Dad saw him, outside, going into the bushes. He pointed him out. I think I saw him. Saw his tail anyway. Saw the bushes move, almost for sure. It must have been the rat. Coming right from here actually, running away from the fishpond."

I didn't know who or what to get most furious with—Walter for falling so blindly into the rat myth, Dad for pushing the crazy rat myth . . .

Or the rat. I suddenly squirmed, quick-stepped this way then that around the edges of the fishpond. If we indeed had a rat—which we didn't—then he had been right here. Yeck. No, god, no. My skin was prickling all over my body like a zillion tiny little claws. I scooted the last few steps to the fishpond, which indeed was now the fishless fishpond. Around the edge were some fish *flakes*, twinkling in the sun. A fin here, a few scales there. Possibly a couple of eyes. Rats made me sick.

"We have no rat," I snapped at Walter.

"So," Carmine answered, "did you want one? Because there's a guy in the village—"

"No, we don't want one," I snapped again. "And what are you doing here?"

Perhaps it was the way I said it. But I had appeared for the first time to have actually hurt Carmine's feelings. I hadn't thought it was possible, and now that I had seen it I wished I hadn't.

I reached and grabbed his arm as he was turning to leave. "I'm sorry," I said. "I'm just, right now, a little . . ."

It didn't even matter what I was explaining. He was ignoring my words and staring at my hand on his arm.

And up they came, his hands, his arms, rising, encircling.

"Go ahead, hug yourself," I said. "I won't say anything this time." At least *I* didn't have to hug him.

With Carmine sorting himself out, I was freed to go and address our other little critter issue. I had had enough.

I marched past the two of them to the house, through the dartboard door, through the kitchen to the living room, where I stopped and listened. I heard nothing.

"Dad," I called.

"Yes, sweetheart," came the small voice up through the small opening made by the removed floorboard.

"There you are," I said, my hands on my hips as I barked down into the hole. "You stay right there, Dad. I'm coming down."

"No, don't do that," he said, the voice coming up a little louder, a little faster.

"I *will* do that," I said, and started marching for the cellar door. I opened it, and even though it was pretty murky down there, and even though I had never enjoyed a particularly easy relationship with cellars generally and I kept a particularly keen distance from this musty one specifically, and even though there may or may not have been a rat with a grudge in the vicinity and if I were a rat this would be exactly where I would hang out, even though all that, I stepped down those stairs because I wanted to meet my dad in his own strange new territory and find out . . .

"What is going on, Dad?"

I don't think he thought I would actually come down. He was there, in front of me, on his knees. He had a surgical mask covering his mouth. In one hand was a bucket of some kind of white goop—putty or

cement or some combination of some such goopi-
ness—and in the other was his putty knife.

"I'm patching up the house with Spackle," he said
so apologetically I felt immediately sad and guilty
for asking, for being down there, for even looking at
him.

I looked around at the trail of patching. Even in
the dim light it was easy to see the nearly glowing
whiteness of the Spackle against the crumbling dull
of the walls and the packed dirt floor. He had obviously been feeling his way around, filling in any
holes he could in the surfaces, mostly where the rock
of the wall met the earth of the floor.

"How's it coming along?" I asked, though not too
hopefully. I think at that point I was trying to make
conversation and that was the only subject that
seemed topical.

To answer, Dad first started nodding, looking
around, mostly behind him, and nodding, nodding,
then back at me, then not nodding, then shaking his
head, no. No.

"There's a lot, sweetie," he said, "a lot, and always
lots more behind it, it seems. It's like there's leakage
everywhere, whether it's moisture getting in where
it's not supposed to or air and cold getting in where
they're not supposed to, or whatever getting in
where it's not supposed to, or heat getting out where
it's not supposed to. Just leakage, and every time you

block it up somewhere, it bursts open someplace else."

He appeared—there on his knees, covered in cellar dirt, looking out from inside his mask—like some kind of shrunken, battered, moldy basement version of my dad. I hated it, and I hated the cellar.

"Do you smell it down here?" I asked. "It's that smell, that wet, burnt-charcoal smell. It is very much down here."

He nodded. "Yes, it is very much down here. I'll figure it out though. It's on my list."

"Your *list*. Your list is too long, Dad. First, you know, I don't think the house is so bad, especially if you don't spend all your time crawling around the most decrepit parts of it. As a matter of fact, I really, really like the house. So does Walter."

"And me, too," Carmine called from the space of the missing floorboard upstairs.

"And so does Carmine," I said to Dad. "Thank you, Carmine," I said to Carmine. "Go away now, Carmine."

"Yah," Dad said, finally getting to his feet but only to wander the perimeter of the cellar, checking for more holes in the walls. "But it really needs—"

"So, can't you just get somebody in to do some of it? There *are* people who do that sort of thing, you know, Dad. Like carpenters. It's their job. You already *have* a job, remember?"

"I remember," he said, finding and instantly patching a hole. "But you know, Sylvia, how I don't like having workers in the house."

"You also don't like doing this stuff, Dad. Remember? Because if you don't remember, then let me point out that you used to look at putting out the trash on Wednesday mornings as a major home-improvement project."

He stopped feeling the walls. He turned to me and stared. Then, through his mask, he chuckled. Like we were reminiscing about an old mutual friend.

It was a treat. I became aware then how little he was laughing lately. He used to think all kinds of stuff was funny—some of it actually was funny funny, some of it was kind of nuts funny.

Nuts funny was fine by us. Nuts funny was fun. Nuts serious was a whole different monster.

"Yah, true. I hated it."

"Good. Great. So hate it again."

"Why?"

"'Cause I don't like it."

"What? What don't you like, Sylvia? You don't like what?"

Grr. Why did he have to do this? He knew better than this. And he knew I didn't like having to explain myself. Everybody hates explaining themselves. Especially me. Especially us. And anyway, especially if I came down here to this creepy place, asking questions, if I came asking questions, then I certainly didn't feel like being the one doing the explaining. Anyway, he knew. I believed he knew. You could always tell he knew what you were talking about because he asked you to overexplain yourself. So he could bunch up as many words as possible to confuse things, like piling all the psychological furniture against his side of the door while your logic was trying to get in from the other side.

"*It*, Dad. I don't like it. *The* it. This. Us. Here. The difference. Something has gone wrong, and it has gone wrong here, and it has gone wrong suddenly, and I hate it—and did you tell Walter that the *rat* ate all our fish?"

"The fish?"

"The fish."

"Well, the rat did eat the fish. Why would I keep something like that from him?"

"Because maybe you don't know that the *rat* did eat the fish. Because nobody but you has even seen the *rat*. Maybe Carmine ate the fish."

"Hey," Carmine called through the floor again.

"Walter," I yelled, "would you please take him away from there?" I finally got worked up enough to leave the steps, to march over the cellar floor that hardly even made a sound when I stepped on it, over to where the ceiling was open and Carmine's face peered down. "Go away, Carmine," I said.

He had his face pressed tightly into the space between the floorboards. "This is a very great house," he said through squished fish lips.

Walter hauled Carmine away, and I turned to find myself up close to Dad, in the middle of the bare and empty, somehow damp *and* dusty, space of the cellar.

"Walter did see the rat," he said.

I sighed. I was starting to feel weighed down by the effort of it, by the unusual amount and intensity of talking between me and Dad, by the weight of the house, which was very much and very noticeably above me now, on top of me now, feeling like I was actually carrying the bulk of it now from here, from my place under the ground, with the dirt under me and all around me.

Dad was hunched over and kind of grimacing. His mask was removed now, hanging around his neck, and the dirt was seeping into the lines around his eyes, along the sides of his nose and mouth, and he looked the way I felt.

"But we won't dwell on that now, sweetheart," he said, and placed a clammy hand on my cheek. "We don't need to dwell on that now, Vee."

It didn't used to bother me when he said that, almost no matter what he said it about, and he said it about almost anything. But it never did bother me, back then; and I figured there would be a time, and I hoped it would be soon, when it didn't bother me again.

But it bothered me a great, great deal now.

It didn't bother me as much, however, as the awful, oppressive, overwhelming feeling that I had to get out of this horror of a place, this fright of an underground monster of a place, right this minute.

"Dad, I want to go now, upstairs, now. I don't care to be underground one minute longer."

"Okay, Vee. Sure. Up you go. I'll be up—"

"Now. You will be up *now*, Dad. Right now. With me, you will be up. You are going with me, up and out of this awfulness right this minute."

I did not need to grab his hand then, because there are just moments when I know I am in charge, and Dad knows I'm in charge and this was very much one of those moments.

I grabbed his hand anyway. And I pulled him up out of that awful, awful place with me.

Vladimir

Walter was still only little when Dad got him the gray dwarf Russian hamster. He couldn't even pronounce the name properly when Dad introduced him as Vladimir, repeating it instead as Flatmeer.

I was always afraid for Vladimir. He was so small. I was always wondering what was going to become of him in this place at this time. We were all still kind of getting used to things. Used to it being the three of us, the four of us with counting Vladimir, who was so small he looked like he would make a nice gray fur Russian hat for my Barbie. I even tried it out. Tried balancing him up there on Barbie's head, but after a few seconds he fell right off.

It wasn't too nice a thing to do to Vladimir. But then, I was still pretty little myself.

We all were. We were all small and young and still

new, even Dad. Even Dad, in this new world we had, was still small and new, and so who knew? Who knew anything?

Who knew you could love something to death? Who knew that was possible?

Who knew Walter should not have been left alone with Vladimir? Who knew? We didn't. None of us knew. None of us then knew anything. Not then. Not then, we didn't know anything.

I was the one who found him. I banged on the door of the bathroom and called to him because I needed the bathroom, and he only needed the bathroom about half the time still, and he wasn't supposed to be in there for a long time with the door closed, and so I was banging and calling him out until finally I just barged in.

And I found him. Vladimir, Vladimir the little hat, was still there, still alive in Walter's hands, but just, just barely. And Walter.

Walter.

I would rather have cut off my own hands than see another bad thing happen to another animal in our house, especially something forceful and gruesome, and so I would be the least sympathetic person to find this, and so I would have screamed maybe, and attacked, maybe, but, but, I saw Walter.

His little round face. He was holding onto Vladimir with all the might his two pudgy hands could muster. Squeezing and squeezing on the little body until tiny black hamster eyes were actually pushing out of the sockets and blood began to appear. But worse was Walter's face. As if he wanted to do more. As if there were no connection to the squeezing he was doing and the dying he was seeing. And so, what do you do if you are a little boy, a sad and scared little boy confused to the very top of the confusion scale?

You love it some more, is what you do.

That is what Walter did. He loved harder, and squeezed harder, and cried harder as he killed Vladimir and didn't save Vladimir at the same time, and he did not know what was wrong.

"Here, Walter," I said, almost whispering. "Here, here," I said, as I pried his fingers loose as gently as I could and relieved Vladimir and him of each other. I pretended Vladimir was okay, cupped him and stroked him and talked to him nice.

And I took Walter by the hand and led him out of the bathroom even though that was the wrong direction for my body right then, and I led Walter to the TV, where I was happy to find some cartoons, and I left Walter there, and I told him I would be right back, and I took Vladimir to Dad in his office room.

It was too soon. It was too soon already for this. We could never be ready for this, but we were not at all ready for this.

Dad and I went back to the living room and sat on the floor right next to Walter sitting there in the middle of the rug with his big round eyes wide at the TV. I got to hold Vladimir and Dad got to hold Walter and we all got to watch the Roadrunner and Coyote, which was good because it had no words, and because anybody who got hurt, crushed, or whatever just got back up again. And nobody sweet and innocent ever got hurt at all.

Dwelling

We held a meeting.

"There is nothing wrong with me," Dad said.

The chair was going to be important.

"Sit in the chair, Dad," I said.

And appearance. Appearances mattered.

"You have to get rid of that beard, Dad, and cut that eyebrow especially," Walter said grimly, staring Dad close in the face. "You look like a villain."

"Would you guys stop talking to me like that? You're making me nervous. And I have things to do."

"You do not."

"Yes I do. Things. Loads and loads of things."

"Get in the chair, Dad."

Walter was very serious. Menacing, even. He stood like a toy tough guy, feet wide apart, pointing at Dad's chair. His lovely and loved, comfy, legendary chair. The old, deep-seat, burnt-red leather chair with the rivetlike buttonholes all over, sunk so well you could only see the holes and not the buttons. Nobody ever sat in that chair but Dad, and Dad almost never sat in it these days.

"Sit in the chair, Dad," Walter said, a little tougher. His voice cracked with the strain of his toughness.

"Mmm . . . no," Dad said. "I'd like to, but I have so much to—"

Walter threw himself into the chair.

"Hey," Dad said, very edgy, then calming himself, "hey, son. Those are old springs. Don't want to pop them . . ." He had his hands extended in front of him and was speaking with the exaggerated calm of TV cops dealing with well-armed madmen.

Walter made his move. He pulled a freshly sharpened pencil out of his side pocket.

"Hey," Dad said, almost a whisper. "What are you doing? That's a pencil. Walter, you know writing implements are not supposed to be within three feet of my chair. Remember, I described the worn-leather condition of that chair? Remember? How the chair's strength and weakness come from the same place . . . like Kryptonite and Superman."

This always made Walter nervous, even at the best of times. "Don't compare your chair to Superman, Dad."

"Let him compare the chair to Superman if he

wants," I snapped.

"Get in the chair, Dad," Walter said.

"Put down the pencil, Walter," Dad said.

"You getting in the chair?"

"You putting down the pencil?"

They stared at each other, trembling with the tension of the situation, for like a year. This was what happened when you let the guys handle things.

I grabbed my father's hand, yanked him along to the chair. I whipped the pencil out of Walter's hand and threw it against the wall. I hauled the little one up out of the seat, and I slung the big one down into it.

Peace. Instantly, things were different.

The method may have been madness, but the result was quite what we wanted. Once Dad was reunited with his beloved chair, his expression immediately reverted to a version of him we recognized. A version we could talk to. A version we could deal with.

"We love you, Dad," I said.

He smiled. He sank down lower and ever lower into his chair world. He looked at one lovely blackened red-tufted-leather arm and the other, and rubbed them and squeezed them as if to reassure himself that they were actually still there like before.

"Now go back to work."

"What?" He almost got out of his chair, but didn't. He leaned forward, then retreated into the uphol- stery like a turtle into his shelldom. "You just said you loved me."

"We do. Don't we, Walter?"

This kind of talk wasn't as easy for Walter as for me. He nodded bravely but very honestly.

"That's part of why we want you back at work. The chair isn't the only thing that's in danger of popping its old springs."

He stared from deep within his turtle hideaway. His eyes, just his eyes, swung from me to Walter and back again.

"Are you saying you think I'm going crazy?" he asked in a voice that couldn't have sounded more unsettling if he sang all the words backward. Walter released a sigh that had a little squeal of voice in it.

"No, Dad, no," I said, because I am devoted to my father more than to any hyperliteral notion of truth. "It's just that I think among the three of us, and with school not started yet, and after the move and all, and now with all the work on the house . . . I just think we might just start to get in each other's hair a little bit. That's all. And that maybe doing things more gradually, with the house, might be the way to go . . ."

"And going to work . . ." added Walter.

"Might be the way to go," I concluded.

He sat there. Started looking a little more relaxed, started emerging in tiny degrees from his shell. Even had a little turtlesque smile growing there straight and flat across his weary features.

"You're throwing me out of the house."

"Dad . . ." I said scoldingly.

"You are. You're throwing your father out of the house." He seemed amused, almost. Tentatively amused.

"We still want you to *live* here," Walter said, apparently trying to allay fears. "We want you to come back, after you go out."

"Ah, you guys," Dad said, shaking his head and laughing. Tentatively laughing.

"Ah, us guys," Walter said, visibly relieved at the lessening tension.

I was reserving judgment just yet on whether the tension was actually leaving or just hiding. Dad wasn't all the way back with us yet, uh-uh.

"I couldn't leave you now," Dad said as his smile started getting too heavy to hold up, "not with the jobs left, and especially not with that rat . . ."

The options for response flicked through my mind. Top of the list was to scream my guts out in frustration. Even though I was no screamer. But I decided that wouldn't help things, so I tried quiet, but firm, reason.

"There is no rat, Dad."

"Of course there's a rat, sweetheart." He was actually kind and upbeat about it. "He ate the fish, remember?"

"No, I don't remember. I can't remember what I never knew. I never saw any rat. And neither did Walter."

"I did."

"You did not."

"I might have."

"Dad said you saw it, so you thought that was what you saw, because Dad said so."

"If Dad said so, then I must have."

"That's my boy," Dad said.

Walter was supposed to be working with me. God love him, he did have such trouble straying from Dad's path.

"Walter!" I shouted.

"Dad?" Walter said.

"Listen," Dad said, rising like a judge, "we won't dwell on this now."

"Yes, we will," I said. "We will dwell on this. Now. I am tired of not dwelling. I think we have to dwell on something, Dad. I think we have to dwell."

He was not ready for that. He stood, staring, his benevolent smile sliding right off his face, down to the floorboards, across the room, and down through the hole into the crummy cellar. He was ready for not dwelling. He was not ready for being told by me that we would not now be not dwelling.

"Maybe we don't have to dwell on this right now," Walter said when he saw Dad's expression.

"Yes, we do," I said.

"Right, then," Dad said, clapping his hands and rubbing them together as if we had come to some agreement. He manufactured the lamest and most unnatural imitation of his own relaxed manner, very deliberately laid it on me, then Walter.

And then he left the room.

I chased after him, just caught him at the kitchen door. Not that he was in any danger of running away, of course, since that would require actually leaving, which he didn't do anymore.

"Hey," I demanded.

"What?" He sounded exasperated and was gesturing with both hands at the door. "I have to get this stuff done, Sylvia. Look, can Walter's dartboard really stay there forever? I don't think so," he said with a chuckle that made it sound as if I had been the one who ripped a hole in the door and patched it with a dartboard.

"That's right," Walter said, coming in behind me.

I turned on him. "Must I remind you every two minutes which side of this you are on?"

"Which side of what?" Dad asked. "There is no *this*. We have no this to be on one side or the other of."

"I think we do, Dad," I said, and as I said it I made a very deliberate grab of the wrist, of the right wrist. In his right hand was the infamous, do-it-all putty knife.

"No," he said, looking at the wrist, or my hand, or the putty knife. "I don't think we do, Vee. And Walter doesn't either."

And with that, when I would not back down—or let go—he did something, a move that belonged to somebody else but not to my dad. He suddenly, angrily, ripped his hand away from me.

Somebody else. Some other place, other time, other reality, but not us or ours. My dad would have never.

He acted like he didn't even notice. He turned away from me and dashed across the kitchen to the counter at the far end where a small army of tools and appliances had been steadily gathering like for war around the general that was the radio. He turned on the radio, then turned it up loud.

I was still staring at my hand. Maybe it wasn't a big thing, maybe it shouldn't have been a big thing, but it was a big thing.

I looked over to Walter, who was also staring at my sad little hand.

It wasn't red or scratched or bruised, or anything bad. Except empty. Violently empty.

I sucked up my foolish girly sadness, I sucked in

the wet charcoal air, I sucked in my lip that kept popping out and flubbering around, and I followed Dad across to the other side of the kitchen.

He looked so unlike himself. His back was to us, his palm flat on the counter as he leaned with one hand and fiddled with some tool or other with the other. His head hung so low that from behind it looked like he was cut off at the shoulders.

"Dad," I said, as I tugged at his belt from behind. That was how I always grabbed him, when we would play, when I would be corralling him.

He turned the radio up a bit.

"Dad," Walter said, bumping me as he reached in for his share of the belt.

Dad turned on his electric drill. It sounded like a trash truck.

"Dad," Walter and I both called out. We tugged him hard, so he had to turn around.

He was all apology. His face, was an apology. Words, however, did not come along with it. He stood mute, with the drill in his hand pointed like a gun at the sky. There was nothing in it—no drill bit, no screwdriver bit, no working bit of any kind—but it whirred away madly, loudly, above even the radio noise.

"Would you turn that thing off?" I shouted. "You can't hear yourself think with all this going on."

He didn't turn the drill off, not right away, and he

didn't turn the radio off either. He reached out, drill in hand still, and wrapped Walter and me up in the tightest ever bear hug. Walter got the arm with the drill, so it was right by his ear. He didn't complain though.

"The last thing I want," Dad said right in my ear, "is to hear myself think."

Then, quick as a cat, he released us, turned off the drill, and dropped it on the counter before stepping away again, to his room, and slamming the door.

I was all but ready to give up, which I normally am not. I was scared, which I normally am not. I was out of answers—which I am never.

But then the cavalry rode in.

"No," Walter said.

He left me, and stomped his way toward Dad's room. I ran after him. He reached the door, where we heard Dad's radio playing away as it always did, day and night.

He didn't even knock.

He burst into Dad's room and went right over to the bed where Dad was lying, staring, wide-eyed at the ceiling.

"Chaos," said Dad.

Which this time was fairly accurate. The idea of Walter bursting uninvited into Dad's room, and for purposes of confrontation, was about as close to a definition of chaos as we would have gotten. Before recently.

"No, Dad," Walter said, plunking himself into a seat on the mattress beside Dad.

"No?" Dad replied.

"No."

Well, that did the trick. The shock of hearing Walter scolding as if he were *me* jolted Dad into action.

Instead of staring at the ceiling, he closed his eyes.

Just then, over the airwaves came the shipping forecast for all boats at sea, something that always made me feel like holding on tight to something or somebody warm and close, and hearing words from somebody who would talk to me about anything other than the vastness and emptiness of the wide world, but which Dad had always, always found to be absolutely vital and compelling listening.

He rolled over, away from us, tucked his knees up to his chest, and lay there like a conch shell just abandoned by a hermit crab.

"I said no," insisted Walter, sounding more like me than I was daring to sound. He shook him with both hands, bouncing the man and the mattress up and down and up and down. "No being crazy, Dad. You are not allowed. We need you to be you, Dad. Everybody has to be themselves, and people can't just all of a sudden start being something else. That's no good, that messes everybody up. Not allowed. Not allowed at all."

He kept shaking and shaking on the mattress and on Dad until I thought Dad's teeth would fall out and right onto the floor.

"Okay," Dad said quietly.

But he kept lying there, letting his body flop along deadly. And Walter kept shaking.

Panama

I had dreamed about getting a parrot since I was a very little girl. Probably, it was the whole magical thing of being able to talk to a creature that was not of your kind. To make the leap all the way out of your world, whatever that world was bringing to you and doing to you at that time, and to drop down into a whole other world.

It would almost have to be a better world, too, wouldn't it? If you felt about animals the way I felt about animals. It would have to be a sweeter, a simpler, a brighter world than our world.

And if I could converse with a representative of that world, she could tell me all about it. About places and creatures and habitats I knew nothing about. About what it was like to be an animal and deal with other animals. To find out how they are to each other. To find out how they smell to each other. To find out what they thought about humans.

And even more. Even more, I could teach. She would say what I taught her to say. If it worked out correctly, I could be building a whole little individual, framing her way of thinking, molding her thoughts, starting from scratch in creating a totally new relationship in the world, and then relating to it.

We could explain each other to each other. And we could understand each other. She would have the soul and heart of an animal, so she would be pure and good, and she would have the words and thoughts of myself, so she would be right and good.

Panama my parrot learned to say one word. "No."

She said no all the time, even when I didn't ask her anything.

And the feathers on the top of her head fell out when she was only a few months old, and she never did anything at all, so she was like this nasty little old bald man with no job, sitting on a bench all day, complaining all the time, and saying no to everything and to nothing.

I tried forever to get Panama to say something more. I was very patient with her. I begged her.

"No," she said.

It was a dream, but it was a good dream. It was the best dream. I even went to the trouble of explaining it all to her over one very long, very hot, very sad summer afternoon, the two of us locked up in my room. I explained it to her, how we would understand each other, in a way that had never happened before, and so we wouldn't have to die not understanding.

"No," she said, without giving it much thought.

I opened her cage. I opened the window wide. I never told anybody what I did.

We even had a big phony funeral in the yard for her.

I cried my guts out. As hard as for any of them.

Ritual

He was going to stop. He told us he was going to stop. We agreed not to harass him while he tidied up this and that little nagging chore, and then he was going to stop obsessing on the house and get back to some form of recognizable Dad behavior, full of the regular level of eccentricities and oddities and comfortable rituals.

We liked our rituals.

We perhaps clung to our rituals, perhaps depended on our rituals a bit heavily, but so what? What if they got us along, got us through, got us from A to B and whatever letters beyond we could manage? Wasn't that okay in the end? Wasn't it okay to depend a little bit on something to help you along, as long as in the end you did get along?

I liked the hollow ticking sound of my thin, tin

oval clock on my wall. It helped me to get to sleep gradually at night and helped me wake up gradually in the morning, and had done so for as long as I could remember. I liked looking up, at the moments I found myself awake, and looking for the time and reading it on its numbers drawn in cows and moons and dishes and spoons; and I didn't know if I could go to sleep the same if I did not have that clock, and I didn't like to think about a time when I might have to consider that possibility. It was, fortunately, a very reliable and durable clock.

I decided that it was okay to depend on such things if they were dependable. Our rituals with Dad had always been dependable. Like having his special pan-fried boneless garlic-reek chicken on Friday nights. Like going swimming every year on my birthday because it's summer and ice-skating on Walter's because it's winter. Like watching religiously together whenever the America's Cup yacht races came on television even though we didn't have any interest in yacht racing, but we saw it once accidentally and we liked it and so it became a thing.

Rituals didn't have to make complete sense to be good rituals, but that did help.

Thus he broke two deals when the day came for the three of us to go out on our pre-school trip. He broke the unspoken deal that we would make this trip, the three of us together and alone, every year until the end of time. And he broke the very clearly stated rule that he was to start no more new home improvements.

I found him that morning, yanking the old exhaust fan out of the bathroom wall, preparing to seal up the opening and tile over it. He stood there in the tub, the old fan unit dangling from his hand, staring at me sheepishly as if he had been caught doing something unspeakable. Which he had. He had very tired, bagged eyes, as if he had been up and at it for many an hour already.

"Then we just won't *go* school shopping, and we just won't *go* to school when the time comes," I snapped at Dad when he suggested we do our own pre-school shopping this year. The suggestion made me livid. He reached in his pocket with his free hand and waved an overlarge thicket of bills at us to get the job done.

It was not that we needed him for his fashion sense. I could just about remember when Dad last chose our school clothes for us. I was nine, Walter was five. Even Walter knew. It couldn't happen again.

He was good at some of these things, Dad was. Sweaters, he was fine. Jackets, he was great. Socks, he knew socks as if he were in the sock business and descended from a long line of sock aficionados. He would actually go out sometimes, on his lunch hour, and shop for jackets and socks and sweaters and pajamas for us if he thought we just needed that one more item to keep us warm in the coldness of the days or nights, and he was almost always right on target, and we appreciated it to heaven.

But your school clothes are different. Nobody could have their dad out there figuring their school clothes unassisted.

And we knew it, like I said, from a pretty young age.

But we turned that into a positive, a day out, an end-of-summer, beginning-of-autumn, new-beginning, all-together-now happening.

A ritual. One started from necessity and living on out of the genuine joy of it. We didn't need his *help*. We needed *him*.

Which was why it was so killing for him to even suggest that things might be different this year.

"No," I said, stamping my foot hard on the floor. "We just won't go, then. As long as this is going to be different, as long as you aren't going to come out with us like you are supposed to and get our school things like you are supposed to, and take us out to a nice lunch like you are supposed to, and let us pick you out a new pair of shoes for work like you are supposed to—to go to work like you are supposed to—then maybe Walter and I will start changing the things that we are supposed to do, like going to school. Maybe we will just stay home and barricade ourselves inside the Gravedigger's Cottage and stay in here and rot away, just like you—one big happy family, when they find us here all decayed with our bones popping out of our skin and wearing last year's school clothes."

Walter appeared in the bathroom, making the whole weird little family scene complete. He tugged on the sleeve of my shirt and I looked briefly, to see him shaking his head no, as if he were worried that this would actually be the plan now.

It was my job now to make Walter feel better, even if he was being ridiculous. It was my job to make him feel better, period. It was my job. It was my job to get Dad back on the track. It was my job to keep things right, to be sensible and smart and centered. It was my job.

It was not.

I didn't want this job. I thought I did. I always thought I wanted this job, always thought it *was* my job. A job that would have belonged to my mom, the first Mrs. McLuckie, and then would have passed to Walter's mom, the second Mrs. McLuckie. Be warm and smart. Be sensible and caring. Be in charge. I thought I wanted that job, really I did.

But I was wrong. I didn't want to be in charge, not really. It was upsetting me now, and it was making me mad.

"Fine!" I yelled. I stomped right up to Dad and grabbed every single dusty, sweaty dollar out of his do-it-yourself-inflicted hand. "Fine, fine, fine. I will go school shopping without you while you stay here and pull things out of the walls. And I will take Walter out for a nice lunch, while you sharpen up a pointy stick or something and then go out hunting rats. And then I will go out to school when schooltime comes, and I will have a whole life and I won't even tell you about it because the only thing you are concerned about anymore is *leakage*!"

"Leakage is a very serious problem," Dad insisted, sounding like a wounded bear. "This house needs to be sealed up tight for its own good."

"Maybe the house doesn't *want* to be sealed up tight for its own good," I said back, my voice soaring above his.

"Yes, it *does*," he said, louder.

"No, it *doesn't*," I said, louder.

I crushed up the money and held it tight in my fist as I spun away from Dad. I marched out of the bathroom, passing Walter, who was all but bawling his eyes out except that he was too busy being a little man about it and so was instead trembling and growling with the effort of keeping it all inside.

"Oh, just stop it," I snapped, and dragged him out of the bathroom, out through the kitchen, and out the back door.

Which I slammed, hard enough to make the dart-board shake loose.

He must have been right on our heels, because he was instantly there, at the dartboard. "You don't understand," he said, and I turned to see his eye peeking from the slim space between the board and the hole that was once the cat door. He must have been on hands and knees.

I looked at the eye, and the eye looked at me. Blinked.

I was going to answer, but then couldn't. Because I didn't know what the response was. I didn't know if I did understand. And I didn't know if I didn't.

I grabbed Walter by the shirt and dragged him off to do our shopping, alone.

We still didn't know the area. How could we, right? We hadn't been around very long, and we didn't actually go anywhere besides the beach, the yard, and the corner market. So the only option was the mall that sat perched like a big concrete vulture on the outer edge of the town, at the other end of the one regularly run bus route from the village. It ran from the end of our road, out to the mall, and back, as if those were the two notable destinations in this little world of ours.

It was called the Seaside Shopping Center, even though it was not by the seaside, even though it was about eight miles from the seaside, even though you could not see or hear or smell the sea from the Seaside Shopping Center and being there made you want nothing so much as to be back by the actual seaside.

None of that was important anyhow. What was important was that Walter and I got on the bus together by ourselves, we got to the mall together by ourselves, and we were going to go through with the traditional McLuckie day out before school opening together by ourselves. That was what was important. That was what was good.

"I miss Dad," Walter said as we walked through the big glass doors of the main entrance and stood in front of a very sorry little Radio Shack that looked like it was abandoned but was, in fact, not.

"None of that," I said firmly, without any emotion because the situation did not deserve any of my emotion. "No missing Dad. Dad's not here."

"Duh," Walter said. "How else could I miss him?"

"Yah, well tell me this: How do you feel when we're at home?"

He paused, searched, decided. Decided on the truth.

"I miss him at home, too."

"Right. Maybe you just have to get used to that," I said, stepping along past Radio Shack down the main drag of the center.

"Get used to missing Dad? Just, like, get used to it? How am I supposed to do that?"

"I don't know how, Walter, just do. Look at me. I learned. I stopped missing him already ages ago. While we were still on the bus even."

"Liar. I heard you whimpering when you were pretending to be looking out the window."

"Liar."

"*Liar* liar."

"Anyway, I was not whimpering. I was sighing with frustration and contempt."

"Hmm," Walter said, going up to the window of the Puppy Palace and staring at a lazy family of kittens, "sounds just like whimpering."

We were both putting our fingers up against the window, like everybody does with the captive cats and dogs of mall pet shops, to get them to put their paws up against the glass. The cats looked up at us and stared, motionless.

"*Leakage*," I said, steaming the glass window in front of my mouth.

"Yah, right, leakage," Walter said, though I was not quite sure why. Perhaps his solidarity was returning.

We turned away from the pet store, waving at the kittens. They did not wave back. We once again confronted the reality of the mall. If that was what you could call it.

It was a very tired mall. Air-conditioning was probably its main attraction, as the place was haunted by ghostly old people walking silently up and down and around, getting their exercise without threatening their paleness. Young people were in short supply, or anyway middle-young people were. A few very young yelpy kids were tagging along with mothers, presumably buying them their school stuff and working up a sweat doing it, regardless of the nice air-conditioning. And it still seemed empty. And as if all movement was somehow slowed down just a tick.

There was not a single store I had ever shopped in before. There were off-price clothes places and a shop that sold cheeses, cutting boards, and sausage. There was Radio Shack, which I knew of but never considered entering. There was a place that sold Irish china butter dishes and crystal lamps and brown bread. There was a place that sold posters, and throw rugs that looked like posters and T-shirts that could be made of the same images as the posters and throw rugs. There were empty shops. The feel of the mall, as we walked through it, was very much of a place that no longer existed, or at least wasn't supposed to.

"This place scares me," Walter said as we sat ourselves down at the fountain that served as the shopping center's center point. The place overall was shaped like a cross, and we were plunked at the crux of it, with the fountain just sort of weeping meekly at our backs.

"Don't be silly, Walter. You sleep in the Grave-digger's Cottage, for goodness sake."

"This is scarier. I miss Dad."

"Stop missing Dad. I order you."

"I hate it when you're in charge. *Insister.*"

"I hate it too. Tough."

"What are we doing here, Sylvia?"

"We're learning to fend for ourselves."

"No we're not. We're sitting in the middle of a big nothing mall, on the edge of a big nothing fountain that sounds like a urinal, with old people running circles around us. I hate it."

"Snap out of it. We have a job to do."

"I hate it. How much money do we have? Can we get giant chocolate-chip cookies over there at the Giant Chocolate-Chip Cookie Company?"

I didn't even know how much money we had. I just stuffed the money Dad gave us right down into my pocket without bothering to count. As if looking at it, counting it, acknowledging it at all was somehow giving in and making things all right, which they were not.

I shrugged. I pulled out the bills.

By the time I finished counting—with Walter right there counting along—I was rather startled. I counted it a second time, then just looked at it.

"Why did Dad give us four hundred dollars?" Walter asked.

"I don't know. How do I know? Maybe he wants us to dress really, really well this year. Maybe he wants us to buy school clothes for the next three years so we don't have to do this again for a long time. Maybe he wants us to bring him home a sandwich. I don't know. I don't know, Walter. But yes, we do have enough for a giant chocolate-chip cookie at the Giant Chocolate-Chip Cookie Company."

I got to my feet and marched toward the Giant Chocolate-Chip Cookie Company.

"Jeez, I was just asking, Sylvia," he said, scuttling along behind me.

We discovered that they stocked more varieties than chocolate chip. We discovered it thoroughly, in fact, by ordering chocolate chip and double chocolate fudge chunk and oatmeal raisin and peanut butter Reese's Pieces.

We gorged ourselves. They were not lying about the giantness of their cookies. We ate and ate until we could eat no more, eating, even, beyond the point where there was any point, or any pleasure, to eating any more. We ate, in fact, to the point where we were now going to have to buy slightly larger school clothes.

If we did even buy school clothes.

"What are you thinking, Sylvia?" Walter asked as we waddled along, heroically trying to wash down the cookies with cold fizzy root beers. I became aware that we had joined the slow-motion exercise circuit, walking the edges of the mall with the old folks. I became aware that I did not care.

"You know you are not supposed to ask me that, Walter."

"Yah, I know," he said. "So okay, what *do* you think?"

It was only a subtle difference, true. But it was difference enough, and within the rules.

"I think I don't feel very much like school shopping."

"But we have to."

"No, we don't. Who says so? I'm in charge, remember?"

He shrugged. Less an *I don't know* than an *I give up*.

We walked. We got in step with the old folks ahead and we kept that step for fifteen, twenty minutes, fifty minutes, walking up the main drag of the mall, left into the arm of the cross and back out again. Down the main drag, up, down the right arm of the cross, and again.

It was bizarrely soothing. The people here were happy to be here, closed up in the peaceful, pointless Seaside Shopping Center. It was temperate, flat, protective, unchallenging.

But happy, somehow. I watched people talking, joking, complaining, laughing, moaning. It all looked like fun. A low-key feeble kind of fun, but real-life fun. I was jealous.

We walked past the music store that sold those Wurlitzer organs that played every instrument all by themselves and sounded like a chorus of ice cream trucks and dancing monkey shows. We went past the Bargain Books store with nobody in it and the bored-looking salesgirl behind the counter with not a thing to do who still stared off into space instead of picking up any of the books. We passed the Great Outdoor Sport and Game Shop with its big diorama of ducks and moose in the window, even though ducks and moose were not likely to buy what was on offer. We passed the jewelry store, the pet store again, the toy store, Brigham's ice cream, and the Giant Chocolate-Chip Cookie Company, which made us gag and walk a little faster. We walked and walked and settled into a kind of numb groove, but didn't get any closer to what we wanted, what we thought, what we hoped for.

Until we got the feeling we were being pursued. I felt it, looked at Walter, who felt it, too. We picked up the pace, but it didn't help. Somebody was right behind us.

"Hi," Dad said in a shaky, overanxious voice.

I turned, and threw myself at him.

"Yess! Dad," Walter said, jumping in.

"How's the shopping going?" Dad said, looking around as if he were the one being followed.

It was the first time in at least a week he had left the house. It could have been a year. He had managed to trim the eyebrows, and did cut the beard right off. Along with several hunks of his face. There was still blood seeping from openings in his neck, and his brilliant white T-shirt was speckled with red. He kept nodding and bouncing on the balls of his feet.

But he was there. Which was out of the house.

"How did you know where we were?" Walter asked.

Dad shrugged. "This is all there is," he said apologetically. Looking around again, he winced. Then shrugged another apology.

"It's okay, Dad, it really is," I said, meaning the mall, but I could have been talking about other stuff. "There are some okay things here. And it's quiet. Nice."

"Good air," Dad said.

"Right," said Walter, "the air-conditioning is the best. We've been walking like a hundred miles without breaking a sweat."

"We ate at the Giant Chocolate-Chip Cookie Company, Dad," I said.

"Did you? That's all you ate? You just ate cookies and nothing else?" The words were familiar enough. He would not approve. But the tone was something else entirely. The tone was pleasant. Happy for us to be happy, if malnourished.

"And guess what, Dad?"

"What?"

"They have apple cookies."

"Apple cookies? No."

"Apple cookies. Yes. Giant apple cookies."

"No."

"Yes."

"Well. Well then. Do you think we should get one?"

"Oh god, Dad," Walter said, covering his mouth with both hands.

Dad laughed. "Well then, do you think we should get one for me?"

"Well," I said, feeling buoyant and generous, "I do have almost four hundred dollars."

"What?" Dad gasped. "What? What are you doing with that kind of money, Sylvia?"

"You gave it to me."

"I did not."

"You did so."

"Oh. Oh my. I didn't know I did that. I didn't realize . . ."

He seemed very sad about this. He looked at his feet, then up at me and Walter.

"I'm sorry," he said.

I reached in and pulled out the money, extending it to Dad.

He looked away from the money, back to his feet.

"Does that mean you are not going to buy me a giant apple cookie after all?"

"Of course we are, Dad," Walter said, grabbing my arm and shaking it, making the money fall onto the floor.

The three of us fairly dove to the floor to retrieve it. It was, after all, more money than Walter and I had ever seen at one time. And with Dad showing no sign of returning to the working world, more than he might see for a long time to come.

We each had a bunch of bills, each crouched on the floor to form a tight-knit little circle. Elderly walkers strolled by above us, looking down, smiling nervously.

"Suppose we should go on now and spend this on school gear, huh?" Dad said with anti-enthusiasm.

"There is no place in here to buy anything, Dad. You couldn't get an outfit here if you wanted to. Unless you were dressing up for a daytime TV talk show."

He made a noise then that could have been *hmm*, but sounded to me like *good*. He said it was *hmm*.

He stood up, we stood up. We each had a share of the money.

"Let's go and try and find a real clothes store someplace," I said, reason once again being my job.

"No," Dad said immediately. He was looking

around again, searching, sizing. There was an odd little glow about his face as he took in the motley array of businesses on offer and the barely lifelike population of the place. "We just got here."

Oh god came rushing into my head. *Oh god, he likes it here.* Were we going to have to live in the mall now?

"I have a better idea anyway," Dad said. "Mad money."

"What?" Walter and I said together.

"Mad money," Dad said, merely repeating the phrase and letting it hang there dangerously while we drew our own, probably literal, conclusions.

"You want us to go mad with the money?" I asked.

"Yes. Let's just spend it. On each other. We will each buy one gift for somebody. We will spread out, then rendezvous at the fountain in twenty minutes. What do you say?"

I was both encouraged and horrified by Dad's burst of enthusiasm. Great to see bits of the old Dad popping up. Worrying, though, to see him popping up over the Seaside Shopping Center.

Time for me to get reasonable, rational, practical. Time for me to get all Sylvia on him and curb the nonsense.

"This is simply—"

I interrupted myself. I was looking at Dad's daffy bright face as I spoke, and I realized. Realized what

I did and did not want.

"Simply what?" Dad asked hopefully.

See? See, that was the thing. Hopefully. That old stranger, hopefully. Was I nuts, trying to chase hopefully away? Sense could wait.

"Simply not enough time," I said. "Twenty minutes? That's not a lot of time, Dad."

"Especially in a place like this," Walter added.

"That's tough," Dad said, laughing. "Adds to the challenge."

I fingered the money. I had a good bit, probably less than they did, but plenty still. "This is crazy, Dad," I said.

"Here." He handed me twenty dollars more. "Don't use that word anymore."

Walter made his whining *that's-not-fair* noise.

Dad shoved twenty dollars at him. "Don't you say it either. Or any of those other words that mean the same thing. Now, who buys for whom?"

"I call Dad," we both called.

"Well, that won't work. Here." He pulled out his trusty little notebook and pen, both battered and mucky from all his sweaty housework. He scribbled the three names, tore them out, crumpled them up.

He extended his open palm with the three scrunched McLuckies in it.

"Pick one and scram," he said. "Don't look at it first, because I don't want any reactions. Just grab and go and be back at the fountain in twenty minutes. Only stop if you get your own name. Sylvia, ladies first."

"Well . . . I don't think I agree with that ladies-first nonsense," I said primly, "but I do agree with being first." I grabbed it and ran.

I was thrilled, I was energized, I was pretty much happy as I bounded along, passing old folks like they were standing still—which they may have been, but I felt Olympian all the same. This felt good. This felt better, which was good. Better than before. Almost practically like old times but better, if all worked out, because we would have recovered from bad stuff. Against all odds we would be saving the ritual and improving on it because, peculiar a school-shopping day as this was, it was feeling like the best school-shopping day ever. All things considered.

Rituals. Beautiful rituals.

Things were all right. I could feel it. We were coming out of it now, and things were falling into place. I could feel it. It was true.

I didn't care whose name I had in my fist because I was up to the job. I was going to buy something perfect for lucky whomever I held in my hand.

It was very cute, and well thought out on the part of the gentlemen. They had both beaten me back to the fountain and were standing at opposite sides, staring across at each other with packages behind their backs. They both turned toward me as I ran up.

"Ladies first," I called before anybody could argue. I rushed right up to Dad with my bag.

He put his bag on the floor beneath his feet, then looked inside mine.

Big smile. He reached right down and pulled that giant apple cookie out, brought it straight to his face. He held it under his nose and closed his eyes as he took a mighty, mighty inhale of the cinnamon-nutmeg-apple-toffeeness of it. It was like a church scene, a communion scene, and it was very real.

He took a great big bite and then simultaneously dropped the cookie back into the bag and withdrew the box that was in there.

He pulled out the box and opened it.

"Wow," he said.

He meant it when he said wow. *Wow* is a mostly meaningless sound, a sound that can mean anything so usually means nothing, but my dad worked on his *wow* until you could believe it, and then saved it for when he needed it so you could still believe it.

So he did really think his shoes were wow. Because he said it.

They were like high-tops almost. Thick, rough black leather with black leather laces and a thick, waffled, black rubber sole. They were just a bit too on the stylish side for Dad, but that was what we always did and he always let us. Bring him just that little bit further up into the trendy area of things. That was what his new shoes did. That was what we did.

"Wow," he said, and he hugged me.

"Your new shoes for going back to work," I said, in case he had missed that bit.

"I know," he said with a little laugh. Not a hearty laugh, but a near-enough one.

"I'm up," Walter called, rushing around the fountain to get to me. I giggled as he held out to me what looked like another shoe box. He giggled. Then I giggled again.

Then the box made a noise. A scratching noise.

"No," I snapped, and jumped back as if I were scared of it, but I wasn't. Not in that way anyway.

"Oh, come on," Walter pleaded, pursuing me.

"No," I insisted, backing further away.

"Walter . . . " Dad said, "what did you do?"

"Shush," Walter said.

Which made me stop in my tracks.

I turned to look at Dad scowling. But he kept it at that.

"Sorry, Dad," Walter said, but took the opportunity to open the box himself.

I turned quickly away and covered my eyes. "I don't want to see it. I won't look at it, so just don't bother. Take it away."

He did not take it away. He did not even answer. In fact, the entire mall seemed to come to a complete stop—not that that was a tremendous change.

And then, it was on my shoulder.

"Walter," I snapped, keeping my hands over my face.

I was not worried by what I felt on my shoulder. I did not get nervous about such things. In fact, I was famous for my thing with animals, and their thing with me, and my ability to bond with and work with and love every creature the world's sense of humor could produce. Like Dr. Dolittle, except for them all dying at my hands.

So the little light, clingy weight of a thing on my shoulder did not spook me. It was looking at it, seeing it, relating to it, and then fast-forwarding to the inevitable, hurtful, unfair, and gut-wrenching end that shook me to my soul.

"No," I said rather weakly.

Nobody said a thing.

I felt it, though. Moving, so slowly, the lightest pressure being applied to my shoulder. It weighed practically nothing. Like a bird. Four legs, though. Or feet and hands. Tiny, deliberate motions, with a sure, clingy grip of me.

Oh. Hell. I hated this. I was forming some kind of mental picture of it. I could feel it. So sweet. So little, so light and sweet. It was light, and fragile, and gentle. No. Hell. No.

I opened my eyes and turned my head.

Its eye met my eye. It was right there on my shoulder—no, it was part of my shoulder. It was exactly the same navy blue of my T-shirt.

I twisted my head to see it better, and as I did, it twisted its head, tipping it in a kind of *huh?* pose. Then it took me in with its curious eyes.

One at a time. Moving independently. Up one side of my face, down the other.

"You got me a chameleon?" I said to Walter without taking my eyes off it.

Walter laughed excitedly.

"His name is Lloyd," Walter said.

"I don't want to know his name," I insisted.

But it was of course too late.

"Hah," Walter said, "too late."

I was a sucker for this and everybody knew it. But I wasn't ready. I really did not want this again.

"He is very cute," Dad said. He came up close and we watched Lloyd move around me with his very slow, deliberate, careful motions. He changed from deep blue to a lighter neutral shade as he passed from my shoulder to my bare and unsummery upper arm.

"Look at his little hands," I said, gasping. They were. They were little hands that he used in little pinching motions as if he were playing with the world's tiniest sock puppets.

"I hate you," I said to Walter as I moved my hand in front of Lloyd for him to crawl onto. He was so sweet—Lloyd, not Walter.

Okay, Walter, too.

"Yess!" Walter said, pumping his fist in the air.

I was entranced with Lloyd, in love with him already, fascinated to the point of distraction in both a *National Geographic* way and a motherly way. I couldn't stop watching him, so I missed the beginnings of Dad presenting Walter with the remaining gift of our most unusual but most welcome of all back-to-school trips.

But I heard.

"I couldn't believe it when I saw it," Dad said, agitated, speedy, nervously happy. But not. "Go on," he said to Walter. "Go on, go on. You'll love it."

Something there. Something in his voice . . .

I looked up at the transaction.

Walter pulled the long thin box out of the bag, and stared, slack-jawed and google-eyed.

"You like this kind of thing," Dad said. "I knew you liked this kind of thing. Something, huh?"

"Something," Walter repeated. "I can't believe you got me one. I never thought you were going to."

"Well," Dad said haltingly, "yah. Well . . . we're all growing up, aren't we? Time's changing, things are changing . . . time seemed right. It just seemed like the time. It's a beauty, isn't it?"

Lloyd had climbed up to the top of my head now, and I left him there. I was watching this now.

"A beauty, Dad," Walter said. He was managing the difficult trick of smiling and frowning, one half of his mouth up and the other half pulling it back down.

"You see what it is, don't you? See it says there on the box. It's a rat gun. You are a little young . . . but adult supervision is okay. It's a rat gun, you see. As long as you have the supervision of a parent . . . "

"I see, Dad," Walter said.

He saw. I saw. Lloyd up on my head saw. A rat gun.

Daisy Chain

More than any of the others, I considered her a gift.

I came out one morning and found her just sitting there on the lawn among the riot of daisies, and unlike most things I found lying on our lawn, she was alive.

She was a rabbit, Daisy Chain was, a thick puffy fuzzy lop-eared beauty with the softest face since faces began. She looked up at me from the most peculiar angle. Her head was completely tilted over, her ears aimed at six and twelve o'clock as if she were listening to the ground for approaching foot-steps.

But she wasn't listening for anything. That was how her head always was. She sat there looking at me with her head tipped just that way, she took a few steps toward me with her head tipped just that way, and she serenely chewed a few of our many tasty weeds with her head tipped just that way. We took her to the vet, and he said her condition was the result of a massive ear infection she had at one time but she did not have anymore. There was no fixing it, but she was probably not suffering any longer with it.

She had suffered before, though. She suffered in a big way, out there, by herself in the wild. The vet said she was lucky to have lived through it.

But she did live through it, and now she had this funny angle to her, and she was fat and robust, and she picked me.

Daisy Chain picked me. She came to me, like magic, out of the woods someplace, to settle here, with me, in my yard.

She was a love. She was completely at home from the minute she arrived. She let me pick her up. She ate strawberries right out of my hand.

Her tipped-over face made me so sad, though. It made me pick her up and squeeze her every time I saw her. Every time. She was probably fine with her affliction, she acted fine with it, the vet said she was fine with it. Except something in me was not fine with it and I got to be like one of those maiden aunts who go all crazy and grabby and pinchy when they see babies until the babies scream and scramble at the sight of them.

Only she never screamed and she never scrambled. Daisy patiently allowed me to pick her up and stroke her and suffocate her until I was calmed, until I was better, and I could let her go about the business of being the world's cutest deformed rabbit on our lawn.

The one time she ever kicked up a fuss was when I tried to take her in the house. The first time and then every time I tried to bring her indoors out of the rain or snow or just out of my wanting so bad for her to live with me, she put on a show of just how powerful the kick of a hopping mad rabbit could be. She simply refused, with all she had, to be domesticated into our house. We had a relationship, was what she was telling me, but she was going to call the shots.

She chose me. She chose the conditions. She was the tilty-headed boss. That would be that.

I would stare at her some days from the window of my room, and my heart would split with my wanting her. There she would be, munching, wiggling her nose, hopping a couple of steps, munching some more.

I wanted more. I wanted her more.

I thought I was punishing her sometimes, up there at my window denying her snuggles.

I saw that I wasn't the only one though. I saw Dad walk by, on the way to the car. I saw him stare at her, twist his head to look at her at the same angle she looked at him. I saw him overcome just the way I was overcome, pick her up and squeeze her and hold her and nuzzle her. And I saw her let him. Then I saw him put her down again, look all around to see if he was seen, and then hurry off again.

I saw Walter squeeze her, too. I heard the TV downstairs again, his Warner Brothers cartoons again, I heard the commercials come on. I saw him burst outside, run across the lawn and gather Daisy Chain up into his arms, and his face just disappear into the fatty, fluffy folds of her neck. I saw her let him. He was gentle and intense at the same time. He had learned.

He was back inside by the time the commercials were over. She was back to weeding. She was wonderful.

I finally couldn't take it anymore. I had this feeling in my stomach every time I saw her. The feeling you get when a secret surprise is making you want to burst, the feeling in your stomach when you are playing hide-and-seek and the person who's it is three feet away and cannot find you, the feeling you get when the teacher reads out only one story because it is such a fine story and it is your story and she doesn't tell your name so you get all of the thrill and none of the embarrassment.

I was feeling like that all the time, when I saw

Daisy Chain, and while it might sound good and exciting it wasn't. It was excruciating, and I decided I had to do something about it. After all, I was the person and she was the bunny and I was big and strong and she was little and had her head tipped over and it may have been a struggle at first but we would get over it and we both knew that I was the person in the world to make her happy and she was the rabbit in the world to make me happy. And so.

And so. I went to the yard in the morning after the night of my decision, and she was not there. I waited. I stood on the lawn, waiting. I sat on the lawn, waiting. I lay down on the lawn, waiting, with my head tipped over on its side in the grass.

Eventually, Walter came out and lay down with me, with his warm, round head resting against my back, and we waited forever for her to come back.

Nina, Pinta, and Santa Maria

"We're having a funeral, Dad," I said to his back as he patched a hole in the living room wall that I knew for a fact had been caused by him and his putty knife in the first place, searching for a draft.

"What?" He sounded genuinely surprised, almost shocked. But he wouldn't turn around.

"What are you doing there?" I asked. "Is that Spackle? Are you spackling again?"

"Yes, I'm spackling again."

"Take a break. Come with us. We have a funeral to do."

"Whose funeral?"

"The fish."

"The fish. What fish?"

"Our fish, from our pond. The *rat's* victims."

He didn't say anything right away. He did some extraloud scraping on the wall.

"Dad?"

"You didn't even know those fish. Those fish were total strangers."

"Dad. We are not just leaving them. They deserve better. Walter and I have decided to give their remains a burial at sea."

"What remains? I didn't think there were any remains."

"Bits and pieces. Walter has been keeping them in his pockets."

"Ugh. Maybe that's what I've been smelling."

"Come on with us to the beach, Dad."

He long-paused me again, but it wasn't for spackling.

"I thought," he said quietly, thoughtfully, "we weren't going to do this anymore, Sylvia. I thought we had left all that behind, when we left the old house."

Though he couldn't see me, I shrugged. I shrugged a long, slow shrug.

"I thought that, too," I said. "But I was wrong. We were wrong. Fish need burying. Come on, Dad."

I watched his back inflate, expand with the intake of breath. Then I watched it all collapse and shrink back down again as he let it out.

"No," he said. "You guys go without me."

And that was that. His voice was replaced with the scrape-scraping of the putty knife, while the back of his head remained the back of his head.

Walter emptied the gamey contents of his pockets into a brown paper lunch bag, and we took it to the waterfront. As we reached the beach, we came upon Carmine standing on one of the sand dunes.

"Whatcha got?" he asked.

"The dead fish," Walter said. "We're going to give them a burial at sea. You want to come?"

"No," he said, shielding his eyes even from the bag. "Funeral stuff makes me cry."

I liked him better already.

"You going to be at school on Monday?" he asked with more trepidation than you'd expect.

"We are," I said definitively.

He almost gave himself a hug. Clasped his hands together instead. Altogether more dignified. "I'm sorry, about your fish," he said, and backed away.

"Thanks," I said.

"See you at school," he said, just checking to be sure.

"See you at school," Walter said, to help him out.

We went to the water by ourselves.

"They were freshwater fish though," Walter said with deep seriousness.

"I think they'll be okay with this," I said.

I handed him the bag to do the honors. He had a much better arm than me.

He nodded, held the bag up. I was supposed to say something.

I found myself shrugging again. I looked at the bag, I tilted my head sideways. I shook my head no, even though no was not quite what I meant.

I just didn't have anything. I was tapped out on animal funerals.

"We are very sorry, fish," I said. "Sorry you swam into the path of the McLuckies. If there is an after-life, I hope you have better luck next time. I'm sure you will."

We stood a couple more seconds. It was a weak, outgoing tide so the beating of the waves was only a minor background accompaniment, and the job of sending Nina, Pinta, and Santa Maria out to sea wouldn't be too difficult.

"Throw it," I said.

Walter pulled back, heaved ho, and the three unfortunate fish in their brown paper bag were out there, bobbing on the surface of a rolling gray ocean. Drifting.

"How's Lloyd doing?" Walter asked then.

"He's good. I think. You can't see him most of the time, you know? So . . . I haven't seen him for a few days actually. But he's fine. I know he is. I'm sure he is . . . He's very shy. He's cautious, always hiding. He's doing fine though, I'm certain."

"Mmm," Walter said. "Okay."

"You really believe it was a rat?" I said as we stood watching.

Drifting.

"Could have been," Walter answered unconvincingly.

Drifting.

"Could have been. But you think it *was*?"

Drifting.

"No," he said. That was my boy.

"Well, maybe it was," I said.

This caused him to stop watching the last few bobs of the fish bag and turn to me.

"What? Sylvia, what? After all this time, after all the things you said about the rat, about the *not* rat. Now you tell me there is maybe a rat? I hate this. I'm all confused, and I hate it. I never thought I'd say this, but I cannot wait to get back to school."

I made sure I watched the bag still, watched the last bit, before it was out of view.

Drifting.

"I can't wait either," I said. "But before we do, we have to have one more funeral."

Gone.

My Walter

When my second mom died, Walter's first mom died. There's nothing much to remember because we were not invited to any of the stuff, and I wouldn't have gone if I had been.

I could have imagined how it all went anyway if I wanted to. I chose not to imagine one minute of it.

So I stayed home. I stayed with Walter. There was probably a baby-sitter of some kind involved.

But I was with Walter. He was my Walter then, and that was that. He didn't know what was going on, not when Mom died, not when Dad left the house in his black suit and his gray face, and not when he squeezed us so hard we were very lucky not to be dead, the whole bunch of us.

Maybe that was his plan. If it were his plan, I would not have objected then.

But instead, I had Walter, and he had me, and that was the way it always would be.

He had a head like an orange. He had a normal-size baby body and a big round head covered with a carpet of yellow velvet. He was at the point where he walked everywhere, but he still usually fell down along the way. He made a click-click sound with his tongue whenever he was busy doing something like playing with his toys or throwing stuff down the toilet. If you played certain songs on the stereo, he would do a dance where he pointed with the index fingers of both hands in unison, left, right, up, down, then at himself.

I played all of those songs, very loudly, all day long. When he danced, I had to go over and grab him and pick him up until he shrieked and kicked and squirmed away.

When he fell asleep that day for each of his two daily naps, morning and afternoon, I went to his crib and sat there. I had my own little orange molded-plastic chair that I favored for TV and for mothering my dolls and I brought it over by his crib and I sat there for the entire hour and a half of each nap, and I didn't care no matter what any baby-sitter had to offer or suggest. I was where I needed and wanted to be, and I never for a second got bored sitting by the side of my Walter's crib.

Walter always woke up a grouch from his naps

and even in winter he woke up with a big sweaty head and you did not want to disturb him before it was time. So I sat quietly each time as he emerged back into the world we lived in, back into the world that was missing something so wrong to be missing that he couldn't even imagine it. I sat and watched as he flopped himself over and lay still, blinking and blinking and staring up out his window readjusting, and refiguring, and just staring.

Finally, after just enough time, he turned in my direction, he looked at me, and he said, "Vee."

Because that was me. He gave me that name, my Walter did.

We all slept in my dad's bed that night. Just the three of us. Dad was very tired, the tiredest person I ever saw. He couldn't talk, and I didn't even want to. Only Walter talked, and that was just fantastic nonsense. He talked and talked fantastic nonsense until everyone fell asleep, clutching each other like a scared family of possums.

Lloyd

He beat me to it. Or he thought exactly what I thought exactly when I thought it.

When we pushed through the gate by the garage at the back of our yard, we saw what we had not expected to see.

Dad, outside.

But just like when I had left him earlier, I was greeted by the sight of his back.

He was down on his hands and knees, underneath the cherry tree. Patting the ground down over a small, freshly dug mound of sandy earth.

When he heard the gate latch snap, he rolled around, sitting down on the ground.

"What's going on, Dad?" I asked, walking right up and standing over him. Walter and I were standing over Dad.

"I know what I said," he said, "but I was wrong. I know I said this was all behind us . . . you think you can put it all behind you . . . you want to think that, people want to think that . . . but . . ." He sat there shaking his head. Shaking his head at himself, with force, not like he was confused. "You can't do that. You, Sylvia, were right. You can't do that. I should always know to listen to you."

I was peering around him, at the mound and at what else he had behind him, when I said, "Yes, you should."

"I wished I had gone with you to the beach," he said. "I wish I hadn't wasted the end of our summer on home repairs. I wish I hadn't wasted the first weeks of our new life in our new house . . . on home repairs."

He shook his head vigorously at himself.

"I hate *doing* stuff," he said.

At that moment, he bore a delightful resemblance to my dad. I could only hope.

"So," Walter said suspiciously, "what are you doing?"

Dad got to his feet, revealing behind him the unmistakable-to-this-family sight of an animal grave. An animal grave, in the new yard that was never supposed to see one of those ever. And right next to it lay Walter's gun.

"The rat is gone," Dad said. "The rat is gone, dead,

and he won't be a problem for us again. I promise."

Walter was suitably impressed. Not to mention relieved.

"No fooling, Dad? That is so good. That is so good, it's great." Walter picked up the rat gun off the ground. He was starry-eyed as he turned the thing over and over again in his hands. It was long, thin, and black, cold looking and scary. Looked like it could hurt you just as bad if you were poked with it as if you were shot with it.

"I was afraid I wasn't old enough to get one of these," Walter said.

"You're not," Dad said.

"Come on, it is just an air gun," Walter protested.

"So, it's just for shooting air, is it?" I said.

"No," Dad said grimly. "It's not just for shooting air. That's why I had a change of heart. I'm sorry, son. I owe you a new present. We need to go out anyway. We need to go places and buy things. We have to buy clothes and food and things. And we need to go out to a nice restaurant . . . before summer is over and it's too late. Or even a not-so-good restaurant if necessary. And I'll buy you something to make it up to you." He grabbed Walter in a jarring neck lock as he said it, causing him to drop the gun. "And I'll buy you something," he said, grabbing me in the same way but much, much gentler.

He led us into the house, wrapped in two headlocks

the whole way. Once inside, Walter ran right upstairs to get ready.

"So, you going to work?" I asked Dad.

He shrugged. "I have new shoes."

"This is true," I said.

"If you have new shoes and no rats, you have to at least try."

"You do," I said. "You have to try. You can't not try."

"So we'll try," he said.

"What will you do, though, if the rat comes back, Dad?"

He grinned a cheeky grin. He liked it when I was challenging. He always liked that.

"If he comes back," he said, "I'll just have to kill him again."

I nodded. I eased past Dad as I headed up to get ready. The back of his hand brushed lightly against the back of mine, and I felt in there—in the touch, in the heat, and texture of that hand—my dad.

"You know," Walter said, coming down the stairs as I was going up, "I checked all over, and no Lloyd anywhere. Aren't you worried?"

"No," I said. "Lloyd is fine. He is doing fine. He's here, you just can't see him. I know he's fine. I am certain."